CLEATS OF THE
COUNTER REVOLUTION

Christ Kennedy

iUniverse, Inc.
New York   Bloomington

Cleats of the Counter Revolution

Copyright © 2010 Christ Kennedy

iUniverse books may be ordered through booksellers or by contacting:

iUniverse
1663 Liberty Drive
Bloomington, IN 47403
www.iuniverse.com
1-800-Authors (1-800-288-4677)

ISBN: 978-1-4502-4761-0 (pbk)
ISBN: 978-1-4502-4762-7 (ebk)

Printed in the United States of America

iUniverse rev. date: 7/30/2010

Contents

Chapter 1
GROVE'S HILL

ON A LONG AND HOT July thursday late in the afternoon, when evening had not yet threatened, in the years between the two Kennedy assassinations, some time after the dawning of the nuclear era and before the worst of nuclear errors, fresh out of high-school and not yet in college, Joe Harmer, the hero of our story, lives in the small town of Pleasant Hill, USA. He stands six feet tall, in his cleats, somewhere between his father's aspirations and his mother's dreams. A short-stop on the baseball diamond he crouches near second base a long way from third thinking of his girl and always ready to field the next play.

"Hello Mrs.Harmer," Jennifer called out to the older woman as she raced to catch up with her, "heading to the field?"

"Why, hello Jennifer, I expected to find you there already," replied the English woman.

Jennifer's blond lock framed face lit up with excitement as

1

she slowed to a walking pace and held out a large envelope to announce, "A letter from Grove's Hill came today."

Her jubilant expression made the content of the letter evident to anyone who knew her.

"Congratulations Jennifer," said Mrs.Harmer warmly. "I don't always understand why it is girls these days want to study beyond their high school years but good boys like a girl who can carry on a conversation when they have guests. So long as you know where the sink is, there's no harm in a bit of learning."

"Its more than that, Mrs.Harmer, there are plenty of opportunities for girls these days."

"Just don't go keeping company with the likes of the long hairs. Some of those ruffians look like they haven't bathed in weeks. Why I'd never let my boys out of the house if they ever!" she paused to survey the crowd ahead of them then continued her declamation in a more conspiratorial way as they approached a small group of protesters, "let's cross the street, dear, you don't need to be exposed to those rabble-rousers."

"Now, Mrs. Harmer, they're only protesting. I've known most of these people all my life. All they're doing is expressing their discontent with a government which ignores the general will of the people not only in the war in Vietnam but in many other fields of society here and abroad."

"With the things they say about the American President! Why its unthinkable that they should persist," added Mrs. Harmer.

Jennifer politely tried to negotiate a middle ground, "Well, I think a bit of protest might do the world some good. And though some of them may abandon their formal educations for what they feel is a more enlightened perspective on the world,

I for one believe that I can better spend my young adulthood by learning from the experience of others through lectures, books and seminars rather than wander off into the uncertain corridors of psychedelia with no regard for personal safety."

"And have you seen the fashion?" chuckled the older woman pleased with the girl on her arm.

"Ha, ha," laughed Jennifer, "some of my friends look so ridiculous I have trouble keeping myself from laughing whenever I see them."

"You won't find my sons dressed like girlie freaks and effete boys without a father. You should hear what Mr. Harmer thinks about these protesters."

"I'm certain a World War II veteran would have quite a lot to say, Mrs. Harmer." Then after a moment's consideration she added, "I'm planning to write an article on some of the protests and rallies going on. Do you think he'd agree to an interview. I'm sure our editor Mr. Ramsey intends to get more perspective from veterans who have seen combat."

"You know Mr. Harmer isn't much for small-talk and he likes to keep his war years to himself but if you wait another month Joe's older brother will be finished his first Tour of Duty."

"Michael? You mentioned," she quit her sentence in mid-reflexion then took it up again, "You mentioned before that he planned to career in the army."

"Marines, dear. He is a marine. Just like his father, and quite proud of it."

"Yes, of course, and rightfully so, I'm sure."

"He knows he'd break his dear mother's heart if he didn't come home for at least a brief visit. He writes but I'd only like to hold the boy once in a while to see that he's alright. Maybe get a hearty meal in him. You know?"

"I'm sure he's fine, Mrs.Harmer, but I know you're right. He should be sent home soon and I'd love to meet him."

"He says he'll buy a farm some day," she said in a distant voice.

They continued their walk in silence.

Leaving the small town's core behind them the violent sounds of the protesters was soon replaced by a distinct crack and the loud clamor of a minor multitude whose merry minds and mirthful miens conjured pleasant memories for the English war-bride and mother who had already spent many hours in blissful confusion watching her boys play America's game. Neighbors smiled and greeted the pair with excitement in their eyes while room was made for them on the benches in the stands and Jennifer quickly analyzed the game.

"That's a fielder's choice. One out! But we're down 1-0. A pitcher's game, I guess."

"Do they have to spit?" asked Mrs.Harmer.

"I don't know but with a runner on first we can still hope for a double play," Jennifer replied without hearing the question. "Nice play, Joe!"

Mrs.Harmer heard the many shouts of encouragement directed at her boy who now crouched, fist in glove, ready to pounce as the team's pitcher hurled the ball towards home plate with uplifted leg.

"Strike one!" shouted the umpire to the crowd's relief while the batter stood in stunned silence casting a steely stare towards the mound.

"Come on, Pete," Jennifer prayed the pitcher would hurl

them back into the dugout for their turn at bat while Mrs. Harmer studied the crowd.

"I wonder who they are," she said looking at three men in suits taking notes of the game.

Jennifer shifted some of her attention away from the play a moment and looked at where Joe's mother's eyes were fixed.

"I don't know," she replied, "they could be scouts. Joe said Coach mentioned they might be here today."

"Scouts? talent scouts? Here? What in heavens for?"

"I can't tell from here but judging from the cap of the one standing next to them fetching them their snacks I'd guess they're with the Charleston Indians."

"Dear me," lamented Mrs.Harmer, "they've come to take my young Joseph?"

"I don't think you need to worry Mrs.Harmer, Joe's good but he wouldn't want to run away with a minor league ball club."

The crack of lumber on leather turned their heads towards the play on the field in time to see Joe make a difficult pivot and pitch over the sliding base runner's upended cleats look routine and still get the batter out at first. With their spirits raised by the play which made a quick end of what could have been a damaging inning, the fielding team ran to the dugout eager to go on the offensive and tie the game.

"Woohoo!" Jennifer cheered at the backs of the retreating players.

"They won?" asked Mrs.Harmer.

"No, not yet. Pete can thank Joe for that one," Jennifer said shaking her head in admiration for her boyfriend, "We're still one run behind but its our turn to bat."

"He's the pitcher isn't he? Pete, I mean. Joe goes on about

him quite a lot. He keeps telling me something about his great a curl-ball."

"Yea, Pete has a good curve-ball but he relies on it too much. He burns his arm out in just a few innings so that he can't pitch a whole game. That's why Coach has him in the bull-pen," she turned her attention to an elderly man sitting alone a few benches away, "I'm going to go ask Mr.Reynolds if he can lend me his score-card."

"Ok, dear, but don't let him paw at you. Why, I've heard rumors about that old scallion."

"Don't worry Mrs.Harmer. I'm sure they're only rumors."

"Be careful, nonetheless dear."

"I will, Mrs.Harmer."

She watched her approach the old aficionado while he still fretted with his scorecard. After the two exchanged a few words they parted with a friendly nod of his head suggesting his assent to the loan of the game's record.

"Great," Jennifer said returning to her seat in time to see the first batter approaching the plate, "he'll let me keep it."

"All that work to record the game and he just parts with it?"

"I told him we'd publish it in the paper. I think he keeps the articles we write," she explained then revealed in a lower voice, "he doesn't know the paper uses the official scorer's records."

"My, my," said Mrs.Harmer unsure how to respond while the crowd cheered on their hitter despite his second wild flail at another elusive pitch.

"Darn it," Jennifer said.

"I know enough to guess that that wasn't any good,"

suggested Mrs. Harmer and got no reply from the girl who sat staring enthralled with the rest of the crowd waiting to see how their team would fair.

"Strike three!" shouted the umpire with a violent thrust of the arm to send the batter back to the dugout.

Spectators bowed their heads in defeat when they saw who approached the plate knowing he wasn't the hitter they needed.

"Its the bottom of the line-up," explained Jennifer when she caught the confounded look on Mrs. Harmer's face, "and I don't think we have any pinch-hitters left because Pete is warming up to bat next and there isn't anyone on the bench with a clean uniform."

"And that isn't any good either?" asked the English woman.

"No, not good at all. We still need a run just to tie the game. Coach is going to get some abuse for this. If Marvin doesn't denounce Coach for sending a relief pitcher to bat in the bottom of the ninth, I will! Because this is when we need our pinch-hitters. What happened?!?"

"Why I suppose those talent scouts are somehow to blame," commented Mrs. Harmer.

"Maybe," she said inclined to agree, "I'll be sure to ask Coach Parker before leaving today."

"If you'll forgive me for abandoning you like this, I only came to tell Joe there's a letter arrived in the mail for him today. Would you be sure and tell him he is to come straight home after the game? I have his father's muffins in the oven and so I have to go."

"In the mail? Do you suppose it might be his acceptance to Grove's Hill College?"

"I imagine so," said Mrs.Harmer.

"He'll be thrilled to hear it. bye bye," Jennifer hurried to say watching her go.

"Bye for now, we'll tell his father the good news when he comes home from work."

The crack of a ball in play ushered a gasping cheer from the crowd which was as suddenly extinguished in the ground play that followed. With only one out left in the game, the Pleasant Hill fans railed at the sight of their relief-pitcher approaching the plate.

"Come on, Pete," Joe shouted from the other side of the field while his friend nervously swung the club trying to forget that scouts were watching in the stands.

Everyone in attendance knew that even at this junior level of competition there were few relief pitchers who could swing the bat as well as they pitched. Their closer Pete May was the last player they wanted to see approach the plate.

"Straight down the middle, Jarvis," shouted the visiting coach who stood a short ways away from the third base line, "straight down the middle. Easy out. Easy out!"

"Come on, just hit this one," Jennifer begged under her breath hoping to silence the opposing players who now jeered and taunted louder than the crowd cheered its encouragement.

"Strike one!" the umpire bellowed and handed the catcher another ball to replace the one Pete sent into the stands.

"Way to chip it! Way to chip it!" shouted the enthusiastic fan who caught the ball and was sending it down towards the dugout below.

The next pitch was delivered outside and Jennifer could see Joe shudder at the thought that his friend might swing for it.

"Ball," declared the umpire to the crowd's approval.

"Make'em throw what you like, Pete," came a cry from the far dugout.

"Strike two!" shouted the umpire.

Pete stepped back and held out his hand to get a timeout while he adjusted his grip and got instructions from his first base coach who patted, stroked & pinched himself here and there in a quick succession telling his batter to pull the ball towards the third base line and into left field. The nervous relief pitcher held the club awkwardly and stepped forward into the batter's box again while trying to feign his own steely grin in a vain attempt to intimidate the man on the mound. In the smooth motion that sent the ball gyrating towards home plate Pete recognized the twist of the hand that threw it and knew the ball's intended trajectory. He launched one foot out towards third base and let his hips lead his shoulders into the swing praying for a miracle.

"Strike three! You're out!" shouted the umpire and the crowd began to disperse.

Chapter 2
THE PROSPECT

"THANK YOU MR.REYNOLDS," JENNIFER TOOK the scorecard from him and skimmed it over then headed for the home team dugout.

The stands were already nearly bare and a crew of two younger boys was storing the bases along with the umpire's gear in a small wooden shed behind the back-stop.

"Coach?" she called peering into the shaded dugout, "Coach, I have a few questions."

"I'm sorry little lady, I told you girls last year, we don't have room on the bus for a cheering squad but you're more than welcome to come to our home games and whoop up your skirts if you like."

"Coach, The Journal would like to know how you could use three pinch runners and two pinch hitters in the seventh inning and not even score a run. Then send our only relief pitcher to bat in the ninth?"

"Did you watch the game missy?" he replied defensively.

"Well, no, but I have the scorecard. And Mr.Reynolds is always very diligent in his records. We out-hit the Ravens

7-4 how could we not profit from any of those opportunities despite the ill-use you made of our players on the bench?"

"Jennifer!?" Joe hurried to intercept her attack.

"Hi Joe, I was just asking Coach," she said.

"I'm sorry Coach, she's a big fan."

"Yea, yea, I know. Give her one score-card and she wants to manage the team."

He slapped a passing player's ass and grunted, "Pete, we gotta work your lumber tonight!"

The relief-pitcher crouched over a large duffel bag stuffing it with the team's bats and practice balls answered, "sure, Coach."

"As for you missy, I'll have you know that the reason all my boys were scratched off the roster by the ninth inning was because we weren't sure to have a ninth and what with the Indians's scouts in town seemed only right to show off our talent early in the game by letting each of 'em have a swing at bat."

"I realize that Mr.Parker," she began again.

"Coach," he said happy to cut her off, "please, call me Coach. You should ask your boyfriend what those scouts wanted to talk to him about before writing your article about the game missy."

"Jennifer," she said curtly, "Jennifer Blaise, if you will."

"Jennifer, you'd be one sorry missy to think that one game in the season is more important than a chance at a pro career for our Joe here."

Jennifer turned to Joe pleasantly surprised, "Is that right, Joe? The Indians want you on their roster?"

Pete nursed his arm while laboring with the duffel bag as he approached to hear the news.

"Yea," Joe said elated, "imagine that! Me with the Indians! With those three talent scouts in town and my game on. They just came right over and asked me to play for them."

"Contract and all," confirmed Coach, "so now you understand why there's a bigger play here than what's on that scorecard of yours, don't you Miss Jenny."

"You're an Indians prospect, Joe?" Pete asked after having stood unnoticed beside them for a moment.

"Yea, Pete, The Indians! Isn't that awesome. I might even be invited to train in Cleveland."

"The Majors?" Pete was awed with admiration, "How come they didn't ask to talk with me Coach?"

"Gotta work the lumber Pete, they don't think you're ready. Maybe next year."

"Tough break, Pete," Joe consoled feeling embarrassed by his own good fortune while Jennifer remained quiet to consider a moment and watch Coach ease Pete towards his car.

"We'll get your club up tonight and see what you can do with it. Those same scouts will be back next year and I got a pal from Batavia says he's looking for a good arm. You just gotta show'em the lumber, is all, Pete. You can do that."

"Sure, Coach," his downcast eyes preceded his steps towards the car.

They watched as Pete faltered with the duffel bag then sat in the front seat letting Coach slap his knee with a broad grin and gun the engine speeding off in a cloud of dust.

"Isn't that great Jenny! The Indians want me in their farm-club."

"Yea, that's great Joe. You can add their offer to your list of credentials when you meet with the registrar at Grove's Hill next fall."

"But there's no point in registering with Grove's Hill if I'll be on the road during the spring final exams."

"You're not seriously considering yourself potential Trader-Lane property he can throw around from the business end of a phone-line, do you?" she asked referring to the Cleveland Indians management's bent for trade.

"Where d'you get that from? We're talking about a chance at pro-ball! I can't just pass this up. And if Mr.Lane in Cleveland decides its best for me to play for New York then I'll be at Shea next spring."

"Shea? You want to play for the Mets? Why not the Yankees?" she scoffed.

"The Yankees!" his eyes wandered off into the distance.

"Can you hear yourself, Joe? You're good but you're not that good. And why would you want to career in baseball anyway? Future's never certain. You're always on the road. And a minor-league contract doesn't guarantee you anything. Ninety-five percent of ball players who make it to the minor-leagues never reach the majors. You'd be missing out on college for nothing."

"Jennifer," he said forcing himself to appear serious, "don't you know that eighty-seven point four percent of all statistics are either false, misleading or blatant lies?"

"Eighty-seven! point four percent? lies? Where did you get those figures?"

"I just made them up myself," he laughed and noticed she wasn't laughing. "This isn't a matter of what's practical! I've got a chance to play ball for a living."

"But Joe," she begged, "you can't be serious! Your parents would never allow you to drop out of College."

"I can still go to College," he resigned himself to agree, "the academic requirements for General Sciences at Grove's Hill College are not all that stringent. Pete got into the program, for god's sake, and he barely had enough time to *write* the SATs. You know I can play ball and study at Grove's Hill without batting an eye."

"Just because Pete was accepted doesn't mean a thing Joe. Grove's Hill is funded with the help of generous philanthropists whose fiscal formulae are determined strictly by the number of students registered at enrollment, so they let anyone in just to fill the seats for the opening semester. We should be thankful that their financing is not based on the number of students who graduate or else their diploma would be worthless!"

"Jen," Joe stopped her, "not a lot of guys get a chance to play ball. Even if I only play in the minor leagues it may still be worth it. I can't believe you don't think its reasonable for me to even consider it."

"Yes, Joe, you're right. As far as I know you're the only boy from Pleasant Hill who's ever been offered a contract with a pro-team but that doesn't mean you have to accept it."

He threw his arm around her shoulder and she leaned into him feeling like she'd made a dent in his faulty reason.

"Jenn!" a disheveled girl in sandals hobbled towards them.

"My god, Vera, what happened?" Jennifer untangled herself from Joe to meet her friend in the middle of the street and help her cross.

"Ah, its nothing. I was at the rally when the fuzz made the scene. You should have seen them when Henri started shouting 'Fuck the pigs!'"

"Are you alright," Joe asked alarmed by her limp.

"Yea, yea, I was just at the wrong place. I knew I should've got out of there but that red-haired girl who just moved here last spring? you know her from school, what's her name?"

"Rebecca?"

"Is it? I don't know I think she said her name was 'Flower' or something. Maybe 'Petal'. Anyway, she kept calling out to the pigs and I couldn't just leave her there! Solidarity, sister!"

"But you're hurt," Jenn said stooping down to get a look at her leg.

"I'm ok. Hey Joe," she turned towards him, "I heard you got some big news."

"uh, yea. The Indians want me on their roster," he answered surprised to discover she had already heard, "but how did you know?"

"Peter May was at the rally just before the pigs showed up."

"Really? Pete?"

"Yea, he only stayed long enough to mention it."

"What was he doing at the rally?" Jennifer asked Joe with some concern.

"I don't know," he answered just as staggered as her.

"He was picking something up from Henri, I guess."

"Was he with Coach?"

"You mean the old guy in the car? Yea, I guess he was. That's why he said he couldn't stay. Or else he would have seen a real happening!" She turned her attention to the police siren sounding off in the distance, "I ought to get home. Nice seeing ya."

"Will you be ok, do you need help?" Jennifer offered.

"No, no, I'll be fine," she said while they watched her hobble on.

"I wonder what that's all about?" she added.

"I don't know," Joe shrugged dismissing the news.

"I mean, what does Pete do at Coach's anyway?"

"I don't know," Joe said with some finality hoping she would drop the subject.

They walked in silence a moment for Jennifer to recollect her thoughts.

"Did I tell you?" she asked excitedly.

"What?" Joe responded bewildered once more by her sudden change of mood.

"I got accepted into the Grove's Hill Journalism program!" she threw her arms around him, "isn't that great!"

They kept walking as she giddily expressed the way in which she had run to the mailbox as soon as the postman had passed and launched herself into the house shouting for her mother after recognizing the Grove's Hill College letterhead.

"And we both stared at it on the table for an hour until father came home."

"What the hell for?"

"Well, mother said we should."

Joe shook his head, "and when he finally came home from the bakery that's when you opened it?"

"No, no, he had to shave again and change his clothes."

"To open a letter?" Joe laughed.

She punched him playfully in the chest, "don't laugh! It was a big event."

"ha, ha," Joe couldn't help himself.

"Hey!" she protested.

"I'm sorry, Jenn, but that's just funny."

"Come on! Mom and I did the same," she explained, "I put on my sunday clothes and mother dug up an old evening dress she hadn't worn in years and we all gathered around the table in the kitchen and took a picture."

"Then you opened it?"

"Well, no, not yet. First mother went and called the neighbors but they weren't home."

"Tell me you didn't wait for the neighbors to come home!"

"No, that would be silly."

"Of course," Joe chuckled and let her finish.

"Father opened the letter and told me I'd been accepted."

He smiled, "In journalism? That's great, Jenny."

"Did you see your mother at the game today?" she asked.

"Yes, I did, you two were sitting together. How long were you there for? Did you show up late in the game?"

"We showed up in time to catch the end. Mrs. Harmer was there to tell you that you received a letter in the mail today. She thinks it might be from Grove's Hill."

Chapter 3

NEWS FROM MICHAEL

"GROVE'S HILL! SO THAT'S WHAT you're on about," he said with a knowing smile.

"I am so happy!" she exclaimed, "we could both be going to the same college next year. You in General Sciences and me in Journalism."

"I in Journalism," he corrected.

"No," she countered, "I will be the one reporting on your great scientific discoveries."

"Ha!" he scoffed, "with an associate's degree in 'General Sciences'? I'm better off taking my chances in minor league baseball."

"You know you can do better than that. The associate's degree is just a step towards the undergrad in engineering you want and maybe a Master's degree in something else."

"Grove's Hill doesn't have an engineering program and there's no point in majoring in philosophy or liberal arts. If I do that I may as well get in the welfare line or apply for the same job my father has at the foundry."

"So what are you going to do? Join the Marines like your

brother Michael?" she asked angrily trying to make him see reason.

His mind wandered off as he considered his response.

"I feel I should be doing something with myself, Jenn, and Grove's Hill just isn't going to do that for me."

"But Joe you have to start somewhere."

He looked away from her to avoid her glare, knowing she was right, and saw a dark sedan pulling up to his house three blocks further. When it had parked near the driveway two uniformed men climbed out heading towards the front steps. Jennifer looked to Joe for an explanation other than the one she knew they both suspected and the concerns that strained his features precluded any other. He knew that these soldiers brought distressing news about his brother Michael. Joe ran ahead and Jennifer kept pace close behind him reaching the house in time to see his mother opening the door with a shaking hand.

"Mom," Joe called out from the lawn, "mom, what's happened?"

The cross embroidered on the Marine's cuff identified him as a chaplain whose most troubling job it was to inform the survivors of those who have fallen in times of war. He inclined slightly towards the young athlete without entirely turning away from Mrs. Harmer who stood braced against the door frame with a look of horror contorting her eyes waiting for the dreadful news that was sure to follow. As Joe took her side the older of the two stark strangers at her door began to speak.

"Mrs. Harmer, I regret to inform you that your son Michael has died."

"No," she pleaded and her tears muddied the dirt clinging to Joe's jersey. "No, its not true."

The sound of her anguish called neighbors out to their lawns as Mr. Harmer's truck was pulling into the driveway. The bereaved mother wailed another painful lament and within moments her husband was at the steps beside the uniformed chaplain with a clear understanding of the circumstances which had brought on her troubling and tormented throes. He turned her towards the shaded interior of the house and commanded Joe to take her inside then, letting their friend and neighbor Mrs. Sommers slip past him and into the house, he brought his attention to the chaplain standing at his doorstep.

"You have news of Michael?" he asked sternly.

"Yes, Mr. Harmer, your son Michael died early yesterday morning while on leave."

"On leave? How did this happen?"

The decorated chaplain conveyed what little information he had, "The last time he spoke to a serviceman was while on leave in Saigon. He said he planned to cut short his furlough by one day in order to volunteer his time helping a poor farmer he had met the week before. It was in this farmer's field that Michael stepped on a land-mine and was killed."

"Killed by a mine while on leave," his father was struck by the irony, "plowing a farmer's field?"

"I'm sorry, Mr. Harmer. They tell me Michael was a brave soldier who was always very devoted to his company. We are all saddened by your loss and grateful for the sacrifices he made."

"Thank you, chaplain," Mr. Harmer said dismissing the officer, "if you'll excuse me, I must see to my wife."

"Yes, of course," the parson watched the old marine enter the house before turning away and leading his fellow back to their car.

Jennifer, left alone in the driveway, saw to Mr. Harmer's truck by shutting the ignition and taking the keys inside. From the porch she could hear Mrs. Harmer crying with her friend and neighbor in the living room while Mr. Harmer sat next to her holding his wife's hand. The teen-aged girl gently placed the truck and house keys on the kitchen table then looked to the oven and found muffins in danger of being neglected. Careful not to burn herself she set them on the counter then slipped out again uncertain whether to leave the Harmer family to their mourning or stay and offer comfort.

"Jenn?" Joe called from the kitchen while catching up with her on the front step as she was leaving.

"I shouldn't stay," she said feeling awkward.

He didn't reply but seemed lost in thought while they stood without speaking a word more for another minute until the stricken look of distress twisting his brow beckoned her to delay her leaving a while longer.

"I'm so sorry, Joe," she soothed coving over him where he sat on the steps of the house stoop.

"Michael was going to be a farmer," he said with a tear plowing down his cheek. "He told me that that's what he wanted most. To buy a strip of land somewhere. He swore he'd camp out under the stars if he had to but he was going to build himself a farm."

She was attentive in the way she listened to him talk about his brother as they now sat together on the wooden steps.

"When I was twelve he spent two summers working for Mr. Renfrew outside of town. Just a small farm, he said, no more than a hundred acres. Only big enough for him to plow and seed by himself. Then with a little extra help he brought it all in at harvest. He loved to toil and at the end of the day he knew he'd earned his stipends. Kept every cent, too. So he said, it couldn't have been much but that's not what mattered to him. You know?"

She nodded pleased to hear him.

"Some people will only work if they can hoard some money out of it. My brother," Joe faltered, "Michael wasn't like that. Sure he worked for the cash but there's a hundred things he could have done with his life that would have earned him more money than plowing an old man's tobacco crop. You should have seen how dirty he got at harvest, he was always covered in this oily black tar from the leaves. My mom wouldn't let him into the house he got so sticky. One night, mid harvest, she made him sleep right out here on the porch because he didn't want to bother hosing himself down."

Jennifer waited for a pause in his thoughts and asked, "so he just volunteered to plow a poor Vietnamese farmer's field for the fun of it?"

"It wouldn't surprise me. I doubt they had any money to pay him with. Or maybe he felt guilty about his company crossing the farmer's small patch. He wrote about that once saying how he felt sorry for the farmers who were stuck in the middle of it all."

"I'm sure they don't make much of a living in peace-time over there so I can only imagine what things are like right now," she agreed.

"Some of them resort to growing opium," he said shaking his head.

"Since Mao's revolution got rid of China's opium crops the illicit industry has been taken up in neighboring regions including Vietnam," she said in her best debater's tone then apologized for her nervous divergence, "I'm sorry Joe. The chaplain would have mentioned it if Michael had died in an opium field."

"Joe," his father called him inside, "is Jennifer staying for supper?"

"Oh, no I couldn't," she protested quietly.

"Your Uncle Bob's bringing a bucket from the colonel's and you have some mail left to open. Your mother would love for her to stay."

Jennifer shrugged and agreed, "I'd have to call my parents but I don't think they'd mind, given the circumstances."

"Well come on in and use the phone in the kitchen. We can all use a bit of good news right now," Mr. Harmer invited.

She stood up, brushed her mid-length skirt down then headed inside after Joe.

"Mrs. Sommers," Joe said to the woman sitting at the kitchen table with his mother, "you've met Jennifer haven't you?"

"Why, yes of course, Joe. Mrs. Harmer always mentions how much of a dear she is."

"We're all very fond of her, aren't we, Joe?"

"Yes, dad," Joe said turning crimson at the attention his affairs were getting overlooking for a moment the loss they all suffered.

"You know our Joe here didn't just get one letter in the mail today, Mrs. Sommers," said Mr. Harmer affecting a tone no one suspected he forced on himself in order to conceal his inner turmoil.

"Is that so," replied Mrs. Sommers knowing the old soldier would deal with grief in his own way. "A bit of good news I'll bet by the way you mention it."

"I seem to remember the size of the envelope I got in

reply for my application to college thirty years ago. It was considerably smaller than the two envelopes Joe got in the mail today," he said. "Jennifer has one herself and we all knew she would. And Joe, probably knows that the big envelopes are for those who get accepted to college, not for foundry-bound folk like myself. But he didn't just get one envelope, Mrs. Sommers."

"Is that so Mr. Harmer?" she encouraged.

"No, ma'am, Joe here got two in the mail today!"

"What?" Joe grinned at the sight of his father's good humor. "Two?"

"Hello?" Uncle Bob came to the door laden with three paper bags, steaming with food, and two large pop bottles.

"Let me help you with that," Mrs. Sommers jumped to her feet in the same instant that Jennifer climbed off her chair both taking a bag from Joe's uncle and bringing them to the counter.

"Its ok, Lisa," said Mrs. Harmer. "Thank you for being here but the kitchen's getting a bit crowded right now."

"Sure, Vicky, let me know if you need anything."

Mrs. Sommers threaded herself past Uncle Bob and slipped out through the door before silently closing it again and disappearing beyond the veranda in the next moment.

"Joe, help your mother spread the table will you."

"That's ok, we've got it," said the girls concerted near the sink.

Joe's uncle pulled the main course out of the last bag he still had in his hands and plucked the lid off the cardboard bucket before setting it steaming on the table only to see it snatched by his sister-in-law who dumped its contents unceremoniously into a clean serving bowl.

"Get the cutlery, won't you dear?"

"Here we are then," said Mr.Harmer standing at the end of the table, "come and open these letters before you get your fingers all full of grease."

He placed two large brown envelopes onto the table and watched Joe lunge at them and snatch them up eager to see the source of the unexpected second envelope.

"Grove's Hill," he said reading the letterhead of the first and then stopping himself an instant jaw agape before bursting, "M.I.T.? I never applied to M.I.T.!"

"Yes, you did," announced Mrs.Harmer with a bowl of fries nudging Jennifer to bring the coleslaw to the table.

Joe hesitated before disagreeing with her but had to protest, "no, mother. I never applied to any other college besides Grove's Hill."

"Then how do you explain this?" asked his father urging him to open the letter.

Joe took a butter knife from the table and jammed it into the crease of the flap then tore it open.

With a fearful expression revealing her own inner turmoil now, Jennifer stood back and heard Joe excitedly read, "We are pleased to invite you to join our student body this coming September."

Chapter 4
KICKIN' AROUND THE BUCKET

"YOU'RE GOING AWAY TO BOSTON?" Jennifer could not restrain herself from asking with a trembling lip.

"Well, what's the matter, Joe?" asked Mr. Harmer reading his boy's disapproval, "you said you wanted to study engineering. Since they don't have an engineering program here at Grove's Hill your mother and I went ahead and sent the application to the best school in the country for you, just to see. Best school in the country, barring West Point of course, but you're not happy?"

"I'm sure that's true, dad, but how am I gonna live in Boston?"

"We'll find a way to get you through college son, this is a big opportunity for you."

Joe looked at his girlfriend's downcast expression uncertain why she didn't look happy either.

"Maybe we should talk about this some other time," he suggested recalling his brother's death, "shouldn't we be dealing with Michael now?"

Mrs.Harmer stifled another sob and reached for his hand across the table.

"We have to go on, Joe," she said failing to conceal her loss as well as her husband did.

Uncle Bob reached for a drumstick and said, "You haven't opened the other envelope, Joe. What do they want with ya?"

"Yea Joe," Jennifer said hopefully, "open the Grove's Hill College envelope."

Mr.Harmer grabbed a piece of chicken from the serving bowl and sat at the table then tore off a bite and spoke as he chewed, "is there something about a scholarship in the Boston letter?"

Joe scanned down the first page of the package that was addressed to him then read aloud, "due to your excellent SAT scores, you will be eligible for monetary aid to help ease the financial burdens of an M.I.T. education subject to the maintenance of the high academic standings which you have so far demonstrated."

"You see Joe, you just gotta keep up the good work and they'll pay you to study there."

"That's wonderful, Joe," said Mrs.Harmer looking refreshed by the good news.

"Way to go, kid," said his uncle shoving him with his elbow to avoid getting grease on his shoulder.

"Congratulations," said Jennifer a bit troubled, "that's just what you wanted wasn't it?"

"I guess," he said uncertainly, "but I have some news too."

"Oh," inquired his father sucking on a chicken bone, "what's that, son?"

Mrs.Harmer looked at him unsure if she could handle any more unexpected news, "what's happened, Joe?"

"Its nothing bad," he explained to quell her fears, "actually its pretty good. Its good news, really."

"Well, what is it?" asked Uncle Bob.

Joe looked at Jennifer who feared his baseball aspirations would go badly with his family.

"The Charleston Indians want me on their roster next season. They might even want me on the bench sooner. Maybe even this season, if they make it to the playoffs."

"The Charleston who, dear?" asked his mother.

"Indians!" Joe explained excitedly, "They're a Cleveland farm-club. If I play for Charleston I could be called up to the majors, mom, play in Cleveland!"

"But what about school?" she asked, "you can't make an honest living playing baseball. Your father's worked so hard just so that you would have an opportunity to escape the life we've had. Think about your future."

"This could be my future. You've seen me play, I'm good."

"No son of mine is gonna make a career loitering in a baseball dugout chewing tobacco dressed in bright colored pajamas!" confirmed Mr.Harmer. "You're going to school. We said we'd put you through college but if you're too scared to live on your own in Boston where you can attend the best school in the country then you can keep your mother company and continue your education at Grove's Hill but you will not run off with some farm-club."

"Please, listen to your father, Joe. He knows what's best for you. What would happen if you passed up your chance to go to college and baseball didn't turn out to be so rosy? You could end up at the foundry." She looked at Mr. Harmer to see if he was offended by her comment and seeing that he was in full agreement with her decided to continue, "Its a decent living, lord knows, but its hard Joe. Don't you want to make life easier for yourself?"

"You just turned eighteen a few months ago," said his uncle, "and now that you're registered for selective service you could be drafted at any time. Which means that if you don't go to college you won't get a deferment and you might end up in Vietnam whether you like to or not."

"He's right, Joe," Jennifer said preferring Boston to Saigon. "And you haven't opened up the Grove's Hill package yet. What did they say?"

"You know how much it would break your mother's heart if something should happen to you. Give a thought to her if you don't do nothin' else right," Mr. Harmer declaimed.

"Open the Grove's Hill envelope," suggested Mrs. Harmer, "maybe you'll like their offer better."

Reluctantly he took up the second envelope and stabbed it with the same butter knife he used to open the first. Then he pulled out the papers and began to read to himself leaving his family eagerly waiting to hear the details of its contents until he finally announced, "they've given me a full scholarship. Without any residency issues I can stay here with mom and dad and study for free."

"You'll still need books and pencils and things but that won't cost next to nothing, the big expense in getting a decent education nowadays is all the gas n'booze you gotta buy," scoffed his uncle.

Jennifer leaped to her feet with relief, "that's wonderful Joe. Its an easier decision to make now."

His mother took the letter from him and began to read it for herself while the others discussed his future.

"Grove's Hill College is a fine school Joe but you can do better than that. It all depends on what you want for yourself," his uncle went on. "I may have wound up at the foundry despite having a college degree but that doesn't mean you'd have to too. The only reason I did was 'cos I spent most of my time lewdin' with the pretties."

"Joe's not like that Mr.Harmer," Jennifer defended, "he doesn't chase after girls."

"We all know he never had to chase after you very long, my dear," said Mrs.Harmer making the girl uncomfortable.

"What's that supposed to mean?" Joe asked feeling his girlfriend had been offended.

"Nothing," his mother replied, "only that if it weren't for her maybe you wouldn't be so afraid of leaving Pleasant Hill just so that you could go to Grove's Hill with her next year. That's where she's going isn't it? Journalism, is it Jennifer?"

"I never said I'd go to Grove's Hill either," retorted Joe.

"I think that if she weren't on top of you all the time you'd have a better mind to think of your future without trying to unsnag yourself from her claws. I'm not sure what kind of girl she is but I think that we're lucky she hasn't sent you straight to the employment office with bills for a new crib & diapers!"

"I'm sorry for your recent grief Mrs.Harmer but that's no excuse to slander me with wild accusations," replied Jennifer in her own defense wary to yield the ground.

"No one is accusing you of anything, my dear. I am merely stating the truth : girls who study beyond higher education are only out to find a husband."

"I never!" Jennifer said too aghast to champion her cause further.

"Well, you never, but you would wouldn't you."

"Vicky!" Mr.Harmer advocated for the girl, "We like Jennifer, remember?"

Mrs.Harmer clutched her handkerchief in her hands and broke down in tears once more.

"Don't you remember what sent Michael to the recruiting office?" she asked referring to the girl her eldest son had fallen in love with weeks before joining the marines.

"Michael had thought about enlisting for over a year. We had that long talk when Johnson made his *Great Society* speech, remember. He wanted to contribute and do his part, figured following the steps of his old-man and joining the Marines was the way to do things. That had nothing to do with his girlfriend or any other girl. Michael was gonna do whatever Michael was gonna do"

"He could just as easily have joined the Peace Corps," added Uncle Bob. "But that seems more like something Joe would do, dig wells rather than fight the commies."

"Keep it to yourself, Bob," said Mr.Harmer.

"I'm just saying, Michael was a bit more adventurous than his kid brother, is all," he forced a laugh trying to ease some of the tension, "hell he won't even wander as far as Boston. Can't imagine what he'd do if he were dropped out of an airplane over Normandy. He's better off going to Grove's Hill. Maybe he winds up at the foundry. Maybe he doesn't. But at least he'll be close to his mommie."

"Shut up, Bob," said Mr.Harmer hoping to prevent his own brother from further aggravating the situation.

"Come on, Jennifer," Joe said taking her hand, "I'll walk you home."

Jennifer took up her envelope and said, "I am sorry for your loss, Mr. and Mrs.Harmer."

She and Joe stepped towards the front door.

"You know its really just too bad she wasn't accepted to M.I.T. herself," said Joe's uncle, "Maybe that way she could hold his hand when he gets lost."

"That's enough," said Mr.Harmer chuckling to himself.

"I can't believe them," said Joe angrily.

"I know," said Jennifer, "the vast majority of women who complete higher education postpone their engagements until after they've graduated which is in stark contrast to girls who forego academic erudition altogether and marry right out of high school."

"No," said Joe, "I can't believe they want me to go to Grove's Hill."

"Oh," she replied, "but you didn't seem happy about going to M.I.T."

"They didn't tell me anything about sending that application. They didn't even ask me if that's what I wanted."

"You've been lamenting the fact that there's no engineering program at Grove's Hill for over a year now. That's how they knew, or got the idea, that you'd have wanted to apply there. Though I don't see why they didn't just give you the application or why you didn't bother applying there yourself instead of complaining that there was no engineering degree at Grove's Hill."

"I don't even want to go to College," he blurted out.

"What do you mean?" she asked frightened he may

abandon school altogether. "You can't be serious. You have to go to college, Joe."

He shook his head without a reply.

"You could get drafted if you don't go to college," she said with finality believing that that would be the closing argument which would make him change his mind.

"And what would be so wrong with that? I know what's best for me. I mean, why don't they just trust me."

"To play ball?" she asked surprised to be defending his parents.

"They want to treat me like I'll always be a little kid and claim to know what I want for my own future when I don't even know that myself."

"But you can't go wrong with College, Joe. You shouldn't turn away from giving yourself a few more years to make up your mind while you avoid the draft and Vietnam," she insisted.

"Maybe you're right," he conjectured uncertainly. "Maybe they're right. I don't know. But I'm the one who's gonna have to decide either way. And they can't keep trying to tell me one way or the other."

"I know, Joe," she cooed standing on her doorstep about to part with him, "but just think about it."

He didn't seem appeased by her reasoning but made an effort to calm down.

"Ok", he said, "I'll see you later?"

"You'd better," she smiled and stepped inside.

Chapter 5
THE OLD MAN IN THE PARK

WANDERING AIMLESSLY AROUND TOWN JOE chased his own shadow as it grew longer with the sun falling far behind him. The weight of the heat of day pressed down onto his shoulders and the promise of cool shade in a nearby park urged him on with its gurgling sounds of water springing from the fountain bubbling in his inner ear to furnish him with further strength for his shortening strides. Along his route he passed the routed remnants of an earlier protest which had now settled into an impromptu sitar, smoke and sun festival. The words of their rallying chant mellowing along with the rhythm of their song he could hear three girls in short skirts squatting on the ground singing the latest strain.

"I once had a girl, or should I say, she once had me."

He had often heard the song on the radio of late and found that the girls he now heard singing its lyrics branded it with their own inviting air that made him breath easier and more freely. As if called by sirens he stepped onto the grass which before that moment seemed reserved for the lunatics squatting on it and with each cushioned step he took into the copsed cove the melody meandered through his mind until, without a thought to the matter, he found himself sitting on sod sipping the rose wine they offered.

"Hey man," said a mop head he knew from school, "there's another happening tomorrow at the square. Time to burn your draft-card, are you hip?"

"Yea, Joe," echoed the girl next to him who continued to sway along with the music still playing in her head, "bring it to The Man."

"Sure," he said noncommittally.

"I love you man," she replied without lifting her head and pressing a joint into his fingers.

He held up the hand-rolled marijuana cigarette and smelled it to be certain of its contents and as it burned beneath his nose on the edge of his lips he asked, "is this pot?"

"Don't bogart it, man. Take a ride. You dig? Get high a while," said the long hair pressing him to take a drag and pass it on.

Encouraged by the girl's smile, as she finally turned to him, he pulled in the smoke and held what he took long enough for its effects to reach the parts of his brain that kept him from slouching. Unaccustomed to the high that it brought on he fell entranced by the curling locks which flowed from the serene siren sitting beside him. Unconsciously he began to sway with her rhythm following the song which had called him there only a short time ago. As the children of the sun danced and played on the grass he once thought reserved for dilettantes and the deranged he now sat stooped over its pillowed embrace in a methodical study of its green detail imagining himself a baseball giant like Willie Mays making The Catch that would echo in the memories of all the faithful for a century yet to come. Then the dream made him a star in standing similar to that of the mammoth Mickey Mantle until his vision tired and his frail frame fell from fantasy into futility with the resounding words he heard once more, "today I consider myself the luckiest man on the face of the earth."

The emotive echo shook him back to consciousness.

Haggardly, he stretched out his legs and discovered he was alone then sprang to his feet suddenly criminally aware of the trespass he had committed in straying from the path. The clapping sound his cleats made on the burning pavement reminded him he had not changed out of his uniform since quitting the game. With his parched tongue swelling inside the desert that was his mouth he stooped over the fountain and began to greedily lap up the refreshment. Splashing his face with the cool spray, he sipped another mouthful and then found himself a place on a nearby bench. Once seated there he raised his head and realized he had planted himself directly across the street from the regional recruitment office.

A folded newspaper on the bench beside him shouted in bold print, "Independence and Freedom From Attack." The quote was familiar and he recalled the effect it had had on him when he had first read it though the words that followed these were lost to him for the moment. Johnson had made many speeches about Vietnam and those words which now shared a park bench with him were from an address which he himself had quoted on several occasions in the myriad and copious debates he and Jennifer had shared both on and off of the competitive stage. These words which he read again as if for the first time were from the same lecture which the American President had made already more than a year ago but which still found its way to print in various editorials across the country. For Joe, that speech had an even more stringent emotional effect on him as he sat there because of a belief it had voiced which had so touched him. A belief by which he measured his own humanity. The same measure by which he held his brother Michael in the highest possible esteem.

In comparison to the weapons of war, "A dam built across a great river is impressive." This bit of truth resounded all the more now after his uncle's remarks about the Peace Corps. If guns are the symbols of human folly as his president concluded then for this reason alone he should feel urged to engineer himself into a tool for peace, and continue his studies towards the pursuit of the nobler effort.

An old man in ragged clothes pushed a cart the short distance towards him. In the fading light he could tell that the man was care worn and aged by the passing seasons which likely saw him stretched out more than once on the very bench which Joe was now keeping warm for him. This survivor of the Great Depression had no other need for the collection of Hoover-blankets which littered the park save to trade for the pennies he collected in compensation for his troubles.

"Are you going to read that?" he asked pointing to the newspaper beside the troubled athlete and gifted scholar.

"No," Joe answered, "go ahead."

"Thanks," the bum replied taking up the litter and stuffing it into his cart.

This same scene could sensibly be repeated on a daily basis, or as often as the papers come to print. The old discarded and used is abandoned then taken up by those who can profit from it by returning it to its source, to be mashed up once more making it ready to be stretched, flattened, and dried before it can be printed on again. The old news is washed and remade then repeated once anew and though there may be more dams spanning greater rivers in yet more impressive fashion to produce more formidable generators, generation after generation will always see war as the prime cause for more print. Reports of battle, combat and carnage clamorously bruited in the largest fonts of all languages drown out reports of achievements in the arts and sciences. The day after the papers press "The King is Dead" will follow another that shall read, "Long Live the King." A tree grown and cut then turned to paste and spit upon by inkers and publicists withers a slow seasonal death on a quiet park bench to be taken up and reborn the following day with yet another story, another crime, another death.

But what of his brother?

It was late evening now and he strained to read the sign across the street that summoned the few who are proud to join and serve but the setting sun's glare blinded him, preventing him from seeing what he knew was there.

"We seek nothing for ourselves," were the words that followed the printed quote. The very theme which had so moved him. To go and provide security in a troubled region, that was the dream that had escalated into a nightmare so many wished to forget and awaken from. And Vietnam was its name. Surely the nobler cause must be defended but who is to pay the price.

The old man bent over a litter basket, a block further along his route, struggling to rescue one more abandoned bit of hope from its depth. He'll earn a fraction of a cent for the effort that threatens to turn his spine against him and when he reaches his home, hollow or whatever abode he calls shelter for the night the sun will have set on him as it does on everyone else. Another age, another season. And in the morning he may rise again as he did the day before, and venture out on another day to gather more in the same futile attempt to stave off the final setting which will eventually bring him peace from the worries of an existence exiled to live among those who have forgotten him.

We make our way as we shape our world and when dusk falls over into night the lights we've created to fend off the darkness that surrounds us stifle out the stars above. A moonlit night may frighten an armed hunter if when he hears the howl of a distant creature he is without the protection of a warm fire, and a man stricken from the embers of knowledge which the printed word conveys is as defenseless as if he were such a hunter left alone in the midst of creatures he cannot understand. The confusion which differing factions bring to an already complicated world make weighing right from wrong as difficult as seeing truth from lie, forcing one to become a soothsayer for himself lest he is led to believe those who shout the loudest, with the darkest print, conjuring the greatest fears to prod him from his idleness and leisure into action and quarrel, for right or for wrong, with a neighbor distant or near.

If fate had written what he was about to do in among the stars above for him to read for himself he could not know but the light that beckoned him forward since the sun had set shone brighter for him now than any other. Wishing only to do justice to his name and honor the precedence set by his father he marched out proudly to where he knew he would be wanted certain that any sacrifice he made would not be forgotten. His cleats no longer bit the sun-softened pavement beneath him but lifted him above his normal stature while boldly announcing his advance with each step as if a fife and drum paraded before him, were the fife but an inner fraternal refrain heard only by him. As he approached the far side of the street, with his heart pounding and a fresh coat of sweat piercing its way to the surface of his skin threatening to bead on his brow, his eyes adapted themselves to the night and his vision became more clear. With no care for the "Closed" sign that hung inside the door he pushed his way in certain he would find it unbarred. Inside he discovered a pair of desks deserted for the night with nothing but a dim light issuing from an office near the rear, a lone sentinel's lantern on a quiet shift. Careless of his vanguard approach he clattered his way through the undefended terrain meeting no resistance until a large sloven man in military attire wearing a loosened tie about his neck broke through the far light.

"You gotta be marine-born to come into my recruitment office after we closed, marching all over my freshly polished hardwood floor with cleats straight from the field, boy," he said with a broad grin. "Come on in, son, you're in the right place."

Chapter 6

BURNT TENDER

A VAGRANT AGAIN, JOE AWOKE standing on a corner with no shoes on his feet, disoriented somewhere in the paved jungles of the eastern states of America. Dawn begged to be transformed into day and shed its light on his new surroundings as postal vehicles brought the sorted missives in bundles to drop boxes on every corner, milk trucks made their early morning rounds with fresh bottles to replace the old and a boy on a bicycle pedaled by delivering the gospel according to the latest Times to every door. He reached down and plucked a splinter through his sock but failed to pull it out then tugged at the fabric yanking off the cotton sheaths, and discarded them by the wayside. The morning ground felt cool beneath his bare feet as he slowly regained his senses and began to recognize the geography of Pleasant Hill though it looked so different in the reddish light of morning. He took a moment to reflect on the same park bench he had sat on the night before. During the long minutes it took for the sun to break over the horizon far behind him, he watched the shadow of a giant recede away from the recruitment office as it slowly made its way towards the bench upon which he sat.

Having left his wallet at home the day before he was uncertain where to hide the tender for which he had traded the hours spent alone with the old marine inside the darkened recruitment office. He considered the world which had been shown to him there and resolved to fight against the evils which bred in the light of day concealed only by the ignorance and apathy of those who stood by and watched unseeing. A young mother pushing her carriage past him noticed his state and made a wide arch around the bench while straining to avoid looking at him. The fear in her eyes looked like malice to him and he wondered what secrets she kept hidden inside herself. Then when she had passed and the squeak of her carriage wheels had faded off in the distance he took to his feet and, still clutching the folded bill in his hands he stepped along the path treading over stones and crushed bits of glass too numb of mind or care for the injury he did himself.

By the time he reached the other end of the park the morning traffic flowed freely by until he stepped into the thoroughfare and stopped time at the cross-walk getting anxious looks from some of the locals who recognized the team-jersey but were unsure of the boy in it who seemed on the verge of some transmogrification. Once atop the footpath running along the length of the other side of the street he could hear the engines of the wide-eyed commuters continue their way eager to report the morning's sightings to their co-workers over coffee. The time passed and when he reached the home of his parents it was already mid-morning and he did not think to stuff away the note he still clutched in his dirty hands until he heard the spring of the screen door screech and announce his arrival.

"Joe?" his mother called, "is that you?"

Guilty of some crime he jammed the paper into the pants of his baseball uniform while turning his back to her feigning to catch the door.

"Oh, dear lord, we were worried sick," she said looking him over and seeing the state of his feet. "What happened? Where are your cleats? and socks?"

"I took them off," he answered without explaining.

"But your feet are all sore, bruised and cut! My lord, Joe, what happened?"

"Nothing, mom, I'm alright. I just need to clean up."

She tried to sit him down into a chair but he resisted and promised to clean himself, "its ok, mom. I'm alright. I'm just going to go upstairs and take a shower. I'm fine. Really."

Reluctantly she let him pass then offered him breakfast, "chips & beans for breakfast, dear? You must be hungry?"

"Sure, ok. thanks," he said without trying to barter for eggs.

She watched him retreat to his room upstairs and called to him again, "you know your father was quite upset when you didn't come home last night."

"Yea, I'm sorry. I got hung up."

"But Joe!" she tried to protest.

"Sorry, mom, won't happen again."

The words trailed out behind him from the top of the stairs.

"You're the one who'll have to explain it to your father," she said to herself as she strode towards the stove.

Joe reached the upstairs washroom and plunged his feet

one after the other into the sink to clean them. The wounds were light and superficial, and he managed to sponge them off without ruining his mother's towel. Making the short distance between the sink and his room he threw off the baseball uniform and conspicuously caught up the note he'd stuffed down his pants then, after casting a hangdog glance to the window where a neighbor may have seen him, he reached for his wallet and stuffed it inside then pulled his pants on and sat down to carefully re-sock his feet and house them in the work boots he kept stored in the back of his closet. After lacing these he strained his ear to hear whether his mother was coming and when her humming reached him from the kitchen he covertly entered the master-bedroom at the edge of the stairs.

Being careful not to make any noise, as he pilfered through his father's drawers, he found a small stash to purloin. He withdrew from it what he wanted then replaced the cache where it had been covered snatching the engraved black rough-surfaced Zippo resting near the mirror in the same motion before sneaking out again and closing the door behind him. Donning an old checkered button down shirt, despite the tear that made his mother beg him to throw it away, he thrust his wallet into his front pocket along with the folding knife he hadn't carried since jr. high school and headed to the kitchen below.

"Why, there you are, dear," his mother said after the chore of cooking him breakfast had given her some rest from her worries.

"Thanks," he replied trying to refrain from upsetting her.

"Didn't I tell you to throw that shirt away? You know it upsets your father when you wear clothes that shabby. What are you up to? You go out all night and then come home with your feet all bloody," Mrs. Harmer sat down beside him hoping he might explain himself.

"Its nothing mom. I told you, I'm alright."

"But its not me you should worry about, Joe," she tried to explain, "its your father. He's got a mind to mend right you when he comes home."

He wolfed down half the plate in the time she spoke these words then stood up with a full mouth and said, "just tell him I'm alright."

Back stepping towards the door to the porch he gulped down part of his last bite and begged her leave, "I'm sorry, mom. I gotta go."

"But you haven't even finished your breakfast," she protested, "where shall I tell your father you've gone to?"

Without bothering to answer her final plea Joe ran out of the house and headed towards the park hoping to find the flower peaceniks he had met there the day before. Unlike the more raucous rallies taking place in bigger boroughs across the country most Pleasant Hill affairs were restrained for their terse term and he was anxious not to miss the pithy protest planned for that day. Walking along the ordinarily irenic route towards the ball-park he began to hear the bleating babel of the day's happening up ahead.

"No longer will we stand by and allow this fucking government to execute the illegal fucking actions which are daily taking place in fucking Vietnam. By burning our fucking draft-cards we are not only refusing to participate in this fucking conflict but we are taking affirmative fucking steps towards ending the fucking war!" bellowed the less than decorous rally organizer surprising many in the crowd who were used to seeing only the censored televised versions of similar events which had been taking place since America's escalation in the war.

Watching over the small crowd gathered around the flaming trash-can were two police patrol cars and several reporters standing by with their cameramen taking photographs of the event.

"So don't let fucking LBJ send you off to fight the war in fucking Vietnam! Don't let the fucking draft force a gun in your hands! Burn your fucking selective service cards and throw them into the fucking fire and say, 'Hell no, I won't go!' Protest or fucking be stepped on! Now is the time to raise your fucking voices and just say NO to fucking LBJ and his fucking war!"

With those words the long-haired leader, whom Joe recognized as the "Henri" Jennifer's friend Vera had mentioned the day before, pulled out what he announced was his own draft-card and set it on fire and then went on with his dire deliberations exclaiming, "Fuck you LBJ! and fuck Vietnam! All of you who are about to be drafted for the invasion of Vietnam, now's the time to be heard! Burn your fucking draft-cards! and fuck LBJ!"

"Fuck LBJ," shouted the crowd while a short file of protesters followed after him and threw their flaming draft-cards into the burning cauldron. Each one shouting animated profanities of a similar nature towards the police and those who stood by cheering the spectacle.

With no less consideration given to the act he was about to do than to the plan that had sent him into the recruitment office the day before, and with the same motivating sense of destiny which directed his every action up until that moment, Joe approached the end of the line and stood there waiting his turn to set fire to his draft-card. As he watched the demonstrators declaiming their disgust of the federal administration which compelled them to war in Vietnam he surveyed their means, studied their manners, and learned their methods preparing to play out his part in a bigger plan. Taking his place at the contentious crowd's focal flames he opened his wallet, drew out his selective service card then stepped closer to the fire and repeated exactly what the preceding plaintiffs had already shouted in as vociferous, loud and vexatious a voice as any others before him.

"Fuck you LBJ! and anyone who volunteers into service now is a fucking trigger-happy boot-wad, no better than the fucking police scum! Fuck the police!" he belched these words out angrily then threw his draft-card into the fire being certain to turn towards the cameras as he did.

"Yea, man," said Henri slapping him a high-five for the papers, "you got it right!"

"Joe!" Jennifer called out to him as she pushed her way through a crowd she would never have crossed had it not been for the urgency of her cause, "what are you doing?"

"Jennifer?!?" a sudden troubled look crossed his face which worried the rally's organizer until he snarled it off and answered her with the catch-phrase, "only what every honest American should do! Stop this fucking war!"

She grabbed his arm and dragged him away from the burning bin to a safer spot behind the cameras while they continued to focus their attention on the protesters.

"What are you doing? You were caught on camera! Do you realize you could be on the front page of every newspaper in the morning?"

Chapter 7

THE DODGER

"Good!" Joe said proud his actions could be reported in the media. "And make sure everybody knows I burned my draft card. Why do you think I did it?"

"What are you mad? That's crazy. How could you do that? You were at the recruitment office only a month ago to register for selective service and today you go and burn your draft card in public?" she looked at him aghast, "What are your parents going to say?"

"They can say what they like," he scoffed loud enough for anyone to hear.

Police reinforcements descended onto the demonstration and their arrival incited those units already present to begin the break up of the rally by shoving aside anyone who didn't heed their commands to scatter.

"Move along. The show is over, everybody go home," cried a caustic cop prodding protesters too slow to comply.

Joe stood his ground and took a stiff shot in the jaw for it.

"Move on, coward!" said the policeman recognizing the draft-dodger.

"Fuck the police!" Joe shouted.

A policeman's bat crashed into the belligerent's brow further splitting open an already bloody gash and having the undesired result of rallying other protesters to his rampart. As Jennifer was approaching to help him up Joe found his own feet again. Shoved aside by the same cop who now had hold of the back of Joe's shirt she dashed after them and followed through the fray. As the myrmidon mandate to molest and maul was promulgated by the violence that ensued, Joe took another brutal belt to the head and flailed maniacally at the air between himself and the cops around him. Winded by the time he was wrestled to the ground and shackled, he tasted the hot asphalt with sanguine lips then was tossed into the corrections charabanc to join the many other protesters who had elected to passively step aboard of their own volition rather than be submitted to similar abuse. Once tossed into the bus' belly the tumult outside, though dulled by a concussion and the now shut gate, echoed with the sounds of the police preparing another reprobate for the same heave while the bloodied band aboard helped him onto the iron bench that lined the bus's length.

"Jennifer?" he said surprised to see her there.

"Are you alright?" she asked.

The portal opened and another bloodstained civil apostate was irreverently thrown into the same cage.

"Smarting," Joe said with an easy grin for his girl, "you?"

"Well, I'm alright," she replied relieved by the character he showed then asked, "What's gotten into you?"

"Gotta fight the power!" he said.

"That's right, brother!" was the accepted response he heard from a quorum of the protest peers.

"What happens now?" he asked.

"Now?" replied the rally's organizer, "we go to the station and get processed. We'll probably get a fine. Maybe they'll keep us overnight. You both eighteen?"

"Yea," he said with Jennifer clinging to his arm.

"No problem then. I'd shake your hand but I'm a little tied up right now," he said making allusion to the shackles on his wrists, "I see you've been blessed with the same bracelets. We're a matching pair you and I!"

"Hey, Henri, did you have your stash when the pigs grabbed you?" asked a skinny pimply-faced boy leaning against the opposite wall.

"No, man, I stowed that at home. I always come prepared but today I made an exception expecting this to happen." He shook his head, "sure would like to know where those pigs get their crank!"

Joe took his cue to laugh from the others, "Ever seen cops get mad like that before?"

"Not in this town. There ain't never been anything like that around here. You brought some solid juice to the campaign. Man, the way you gave it to that fucking pig shouting 'Fuck the Police' straight in his face. Now that's the way to fucking make yourself heard!"

"You said it, brother!" repeated his satellites compelled to find seats or risk tumbling to the ground as the bus began to move away from the scene of the day's happening.

"Round and round she goes, where it'll stop? nobody knows! Will today's contestants win a month's lodging at the county correctional with complementary delousing shampoo, powdered tooth-paste & communal showers, or," the lanky joker on a nearby bench rattled off in an ad-lib game-show fashion, "will they settle for finger-prints & a portrait, courtesy of the Pleasant Hill community police department?"

"Stay tuned and find out right after the break!" Henri added in the same humorous tone.

They bounced along with the bus uncertain of their destination but gaining a sense of camaraderie from the ride.

"Hey man," Henri began anew, "you know what the single most often printed phrase in the english language is?"

"Close cover before striking," suggested Jennifer.

"No, man," Henri said disappointed.

"You are here?" offered another, "like on the maps?"

"No, man, its 'No Trespassing'," Henri confirmed, "the single most often printed phrase in the english language is 'no fucking trespassing'. I mean, can you believe that? Not 'Get well soon', 'free meal' or 'I love you'. The one phrase which we gotta see most often is 'no fucking trespassing'!"

"All people care about is their property," agreed one of the girls sitting further towards the back raising her voice above the rattle of the bus, "if it isn't their house or car its their tv sets and stereos."

"When you got nothin', you got nothin' to lose!" sang the joker.

The revered phrase caused smiles all around and another one asked, "anyone here pick up a copy of Dylan's latest album?"

"Blonde on Blonde?" "I did" "So did I," were some of the replies to this inquiry.

"You like Dylan right," Henri asked Joe.

"Sure, who doesn't?" he replied.

"And you?" the question was turned towards Jennifer, "you like Dylan too, right? 'cos my roomies and I are throwing a little party to celebrate today's happening and we'd all like for you to come."

"I don't know," she said reluctantly, "I have to be at work tomorrow."

"Sure," Joe agreed for her, "we wouldn't miss it."

"but," Jennifer began and was interrupted when the bus stopped.

"We're here," said Henri.

"Where's here?" asked another.

"Prints & a photo," said the lanky jokester gleefully laughing, "who hasn't been here before?"

"Joe?" Jennifer whimpered with worry.

The gate was opened and a police sergeant addressed them, "You are now at the Pleasant Hill Police Department where you are to be processed for arraignment. When you are called upon you will proceed to disembark from the corrections vehicle in an orderly fashion. There will be no shouting or fighting. Should you, for any reason, appear to be a risk to yourself or to those around you you will immediately be restrained and moved to isolation. Remain seated until you are ordered to step forward and be processed."

"Could I get a criminal record for this?" Jennifer asked with some concern, "what will I tell my parents?"

"You can fight it," said a girl beside her.

"Think of it as a life-experience, Jenn," Joe said trying to ease her worries, "this way you'll have a personal point of reference when you report on those who are wrongly incarcerated."

Henri listened to them and was surprised by the language he heard.

"You two go to school or somethin'?"

"Yes," Jennifer replied proudly, "I study journalism."

"Journalism? where at?"

"I'll start Grove's Hill College in september," she explained as the thought distracted her from her current situation.

"So you're not actually studying journalism right now, then?"

"No, its the holidays but I've been a jr. reporter for The Herald for over a year now."

"Pleasant Hill Herald?" asked another girl agreeably, "are you Jennifer Blaise?"

"Yes," she replied with some surprise, "you've read my articles?"

"Some," answered the slight red-head, "I just moved here only a short while ago but I remember reading your article about the Pleasant Hill town flag. Do you write them yourself or are they edited for you?"

"They rarely publish an entire article. I mean some of the older writers who have their own columns are left pretty much to themselves, I imagine, but what gets written is most often chopped to fit the page limitations which are determined by budgetary needs and the paper's allocated advertisement space," she said then hesitated to admit, "and I often have to resubmit several times before it goes to print if it reaches cut'n paste at all."

"But you write every word in your articles?"

"Yes," Jennifer was glad to speak to someone with whom she could relate, "the assignments they've given me have been quite varied. Its hard work but its always a lot of fun."

"Alright, girls! Four more," said the police sergeant.

Without looking to Joe, Jennifer filed off the bus with her new friend and the gate slammed shut once more. When all the girls had gone, the boys relaxed in their absence.

"How do you like the ass on that Charlotte?" asked one.

"The brunette there with the tits?" Henri rejoined.

"That's the one," said the other.

"Keep it down in there!" shouted a constable crashing his baton into the side of the bus.

"Fuck you pig!" was the lanky's fellow's bellowed riposte.

The gate flew opened and two officers, who had been eagerly waiting for the occasion to attack, lunged inside with swinging night-sticks not caring who they struck while two more followed after them covering their retreat as the vanguard bloodied the bus and snatched the one who had heralded their assault with his vexing invitation. Taking his punches to prove that he was there and earning a second scar for later boasts, Joe made a fettered effort to repel their attack and was himself thrown aside, kicked and leveled so that it was not until the gate had shut them up again before he could stagger to his feet.

"Ah, fuck!" he complained and sat on the bench worried about his wrists.

"Fucking pigs, eh!" added another who was bleeding from the mouth.

They lamented quietly for fear of another impromptu lesson until Henri asked, "Hey, Joe, that girl of yours, she really writes? In the paper?"

"Yea," Joe confirmed still wincing about his wrists, "why?"

"She should write about the cause, man. Help stop this fucking war."

"I'm sure she'd love to get an interview," Joe answered trying not to cringe as he spoke, "I'll bring her over, you can talk to her."

Henri nodded with a glow on his face eager to follow through with this plan adding, "only we should wait until I get back."

"Back? what you won't be around?" Joe asked.

"Henri?" an anxious acolyte interrupted, "he doesn't need to know about that."

"Chill, man," Henri rebuked him, "just chill alright. This guy's got a bloody jaw just like the rest of us! So chill out! Alright!?"

"I'm just sayin', we don't need anyone getting in on our thing here."

Henri's glare was enough to push him off.

"I'll be out of town for a couple of weeks to pick up a friend on the west coast."

"Another crank run, eh Henri?" asked the same skinny pimply-faced boy as before.

"Shut up, man," hissed the other, "we don't even know this guy."

"Hey, its cool," Joe declared in the common cant to ease their fears, "I won't say nothin'. I wouldn't have no one to say nothin' to no how."

The gate opened again.

"Now we get to you assholes!" said the police constable, "four of you fucking draft-dodging faggots get off my bus!"

Chapter 8

Prints and a Photo

———————————————

Joe found himself continuing his education in a holding cell the size of a small classroom. Three concrete walls held three benches along their breadths and in the cell with him, aside from a dirty toilet in the corner hidden behind a hip-high extension of concrete, were the drubbed dreg demonstrators of the day. The iron bars that made up the fourth wall, long polished by nervous hands that clung to them while waiting to escape the confines of their cage, extended from one end of the holding area to the other while the girls, heard but not seen, loitered about in an adjacent cell which Jennifer had earlier reported was considerably smaller than his own though the conversations she was having with the girls there were livelier and more eloquent than the gloomy gab or boisterous bravado pawned as palaver among his fellow draft-delinquent detainees.

"Blaise, Jennifer," he heard a constable call her to the gate.

"Yes, officer," she replied nervously.

Joe strained to hear what they were saying and came to

understand that her employer at The Herald had reasoned with the D.A.'s office to drop the charges against her. She was free to go.

"Will my parents be notified of my arrest?" she asked while being let out of her cell.

"Not by the police department, ma'am. Not today," said the constable escorting her to the desk around the corner where she disappeared still probing him for more information about what would follow.

"And when can I retrieve my notes," she asked, "was the Herald's cameraman arrested too?"

"Did you see him in the bus with you?"

Their conversation was more difficult to hear now, and though Joe struggled to discern the rest of what was said he no longer had reason to worry about her as he knew that she would be fine. Letting a grin creep onto his face he turned towards the others beside him and listened to the dogmatic democracy, socialist assertions and anarchist axioms which they disgorged undigested.

One by one, they were called to the gate and their numbers dwindled until three were left and no one any longer felt the need to pronounce their presence with any further blustery blather.

Joe was called out next.

"Harmer, Joe!"

"here," he replied in a resigned tone.

"You're up," said the policeman unbarring the way.

Having been stripped of their laces his boots made him shuffle rather than walk towards the uniformed lawful abettor who stood by ensuring the draft-dodging coward not grow guts and dare a dash for the door once the gate was opened.

Joe was escorted to a tall counter behind which another officer sat whose job it was to release, arraign or detain according to the district attorney's whims and the warrants pertaining to the matter before him. Standing atop the worn remnants of a faded red line painted on the floor Joe waited for instructions and surveyed his surroundings realizing he was still inside a restricted part of the police station unsure whether he was to be manacled for remand or freed to walk on a promise to appear. Barring the thought of a negligible fine, which would be more insulting than lenient, he considered upping the ante with a well invented slur then heard the sergeant at the desk address him.

"Are you Joe Harmer?"

"yea."

"You're being charged with one count of disturbing the peace and a failure to possess a selective service registration card…"

"What?" Joe cut him off, "Since when is that a crime?"

"Since 1942! Didn't your father ever tell ya? Says so right on the card if you'd've bothered to read yours before burning it. *You are required to have this card in your possession at all times.*"

Getting no reply from Joe except for the befuddled and astonished look on his face, the constable continued, "You will have to appear before a judge to answer for the charges which have been brought again you, should you fail to appear a warrant will be issued for your arress. Do you understand these instructions?" he droned off.

"Sure. Court. Whatever," Joe replied with disenchantment, "and when is this court date?"

"Week from tuesday," said the sergeant handing him an

official type written notice, "its your responsibility to contact a lawyer."

"Yea, yea," Joe said dismissively, "what about my stuff?"

The policeman pulled a large brown envelope from the side of his desk. He examined the last name and record number written on it to be certain he had the right one, then proceeded to empty its contents on the counter enumerating the items off of a corresponding list and announcing them aloud. Joe collected his bills, cards and papers and packed them into his wallet. Once he had stuffed his library card, expired student ID and driver's license into a side flap he grabbed the coins returned to him and jammed them in his left pocket along with the wallet. Next he was offered the knife he had owned since his junior year. He opened the blade to see if it had not been damaged then concealed it in his other pocket. In the intervening time his boot-laces had appeared on the edge of the counter. He took these and, seeing the empty brown envelope being discarded to the side he waited a moment before asking, "what about my lighter?"

"What? You think you're gonna need to burn another draft-card any time soon?" asked the cop.

"How would you know what I burn?" he defied.

"Joe Harmer?" the constable said leaning forward, "You played with my boy Tommy in the American Legion Baseball League, ain't ya?"

"I don't know no 'Tommy' but I played ball, yea. What of it?"

"And your pa, he's a member of the Legion, along with that English gal', your momma, now isn't he?"

"What of it?" Joe repeated getting an inclination of where this was going.

"I don't recall when las' I set to talk to your pa, boy, but it seem to me he'd be a might interest in hearing what use you made of the lighter he carried with'em up the beaches of Normandy!" explained the veteran. "I know its his lighter on account its got his name wrote on it. So's you jus' gonna have to trust me to give it to'em when next I sees him at the Legion a'fore he figures what you've done with it."

"I'll give it back to him myself," Joe asserted placing his hand flat onto the counter and threatening to make a problem.

Reluctant to trust Joe to do what he promised the sergeant said, "When next I to see your pa at the Legion, boy, it'd be best if he weren't scratching the side of a match box for his light, else I reckon I might be inclined to have you picked up agin', you understand me?"

Joe took the lighter, read the engraved name and stowed it away with a disgruntled but passive, "Yea, boss, I got it."

"Another one ready for ya, Marty," said the old police officer to the cop standing next to the door.

"Alright, Joe," he said leading him to a thick locked barrier. Opening the door he explained, "turn left at the end of the hall, down one flight and you'll find yourself in the lobby of the Pleasant Hill Police Department on Main Street."

"Thanks," Joe replied surprised by the courtesy he was offered remembering the earlier violence he had suffered at the hands of this man's colleagues.

Following those simple instructions carried him along a corridor, past a large open office with several desks and two smaller stations, beyond which he found a firewall between himself and the promised stairwell leading to the lobby below.

He played with his father's Zippo, testing its flame, while singing under his breath.

"… biding my time, drinking her wine."

"Joe," Jennifer called out to him from the lobby, "are you alright?"

She stood and greeted him with a curt hug then invited him to sit with her.

"Sure, Jenn, I'm alright. Thought my wrists were gonna fall off for a while but I'm alright, now. How about you?" he asked showing concern, "did you get your notes back?"

"Yes," she snatched them off the table beside her, "intact! Brett, the cameraman that was at the demonstration with me, called Mr.Ricci at the office when he saw me put into the bus. I haven't had a chance to thank him yet but the officer told me that its because of him that the offense of 'disturbing the peace' they were threatening to hold me with was dropped."

She reached for his hands looking for fingerprint ink and found none.

"No fingerprints either?" she asked pleasantly surprised after a cursory look, "they're not charging you?"

"No, no," he said, "they took my prints. Prints & a portrait, remember? Almost kept my lighter too."

"Is that yours?" she asked distracted by his assertion then resumed her interrogation pushing the lighter aside nearly burning herself in the process, "what did they charge you with? Did you have to post bail?"

"They charged me with 'failure to possess a selective service registration card'," he said sounding disgusted, "can you believe it?"

"Yea," she answered, "I wouldn't have believed it but thats what some of the others said too. That and disturbing the peace. I'm surprised they didn't charge you with assault or resisting arresting because of the way you were swinging at them before they handcuffed you."

"I suppose," he said without concern, "they did charge me with disturbing the peace, though. I have to go to court tuesday next, he said."

"Ethyl," they turned their heads to see her father call after his wife who lagged somewhere behind him, "I've found her. She's over here."

Mr.Blaise stormed in from the door and Jennifer stood in a panic having never seen him so upset. She took up her notes and side stepped around the table to get between him and the boy he held responsible for her arrest.

"Daddy, please don't!" she begged hoping to prevent him from getting closer to Joe.

"How dare you get my little girl in trouble with the law?" Mr.Blaise shoved Jennifer aside to take a swing at Joe.

"Daddy, please! Stop!"

Police officers jumped in before Mr.Blaise could take another swing at the boy who was agile enough to dodge the first and shun the second.

"Jennifer! Are you alright," Mrs.Blaise called to her daughter without seeing or hearing the state of the girl's father.

"Go, Joe," she said exhorting him to leave, "just go. I'll call you later."

"Oh, no, you won't," her father declared as the constables eased their hold of him, "you're grounded!"

"Daddy, I'm eighteen!"

"Are you alright?" her mother asked seeing that she was and holding her with a sense of relief.

"Yes, mother. It was nothing. It wasn't Joe's fault. Really," she entreated with her parents, "its ok. I'm fine."

Seeing that Jennifer was not in any danger, Joe took the first police officer's suggestion and started towards the door mouthing the words, "I'll stop by," to the backs of Mr. and Mrs. Blaise. His girlfriend nodded her understanding and smiled more easily at her father who was already beginning to calm down.

With the cool evening air greeting him, Joe's mind strayed as thoughts of crank, and his next diversion distracted him away from the moment.

Chapter 9

HALL OF THE FREE LOVE FAITH

THE NIGHTLIFE IN PLEASANT HILL on a friday night was not something which Joe had ever been in the habit of exploring and so it was with fresh scars and a torn button-down shirt that he ventured for the first time towards the more vulgar avenues of this quiet and otherwise chaste little town. Already, from a distance, he began to hear the faint rhythm of urchin ceremonies summoning the nuclear age's first progeny to its seditious estate. The discordant half-heard beats that echoed from building to building awakened in him primal tendencies which evolution had neglected to erase. Drawn by the pulsating chords and rebellious vocal discharges of angry youths armed with electric guitars that cried out for him to count himself among the children of discontent, he snubbed the old stained-wood doors of the quiet tavern where drunken men leering at flickering screens rotted, and continued apace towards the euphonious harmonies that called him forward. A strident guitar's melodious wail reached his uninitiated ears while an English epicurean ingénue's muffled voice filtered its way through the walls of the town's dance hall, sanctuary for the

64

local defecting conclave to gyrate chaperon-free beneath a concealing smoke-filled darkness.

The clamor inside made the pavement beneath him vibrate as it carped its captivity and then burst forth and rang out with a slender girl's push of the door. She fell through and out allowing the melody's infectious throb to strike him where he stood. More beautiful than any goddess of the silver screen, the sheen of sweat on her neck gleamed in the glow of the night's neon light as a testimony to her cadence creed. The elation of her features was like an air-borne disease which affected anyone attacked by her starry entrancing stare with a seraphic symptom of euphoria.

"Hi," she said, "you got a joint?"

The promise that she may totter onto him urged him to step closer and give her support. She discovered his shoulder while the music inside the dance hall paused between songs then started up again and in a moment two girls, followed by three boys in complement to their party, issued out after them.

"Cornelia," laughed one girl in as terminal a state of transient enchantment as her friend, "we thought we'd lost you!"

The boys filed past Joe without seeing him and headed towards the back of the building

Nudging her friend along she whispered a conspiracy into her ear, "Come on."

"See ya," breathed Joe's familiar stranger.

"See ya," he said, a reformed neophyte of the free love faith.

He watched the pair stumble away following after the boys then looked towards the dance hall once more and heard the opening chords of The Sound of Silence. Pulling the door open he let the revolution leak out for a moment then shut it in again to see that the dimly lit dance floor was barren while the smoky room thronged with revelers in various states of consciousness.

"Hello darkness my old friend…"

He recognized the song, having heard it on a distant radio some time ago. But had never experienced it before now as its clamorous quiescence energized a more placid understanding. An idea, brought on like a flash of light and germinating since he found himself bare-socked on the corner that morning, recalled the images of politicians fielding benign questions without answering anything at all and leaving television audiences distractedly awaiting the start of a more entertaining commercial program.

"Fools!" the duo sang out through the hall and a cancer crept in along with him as he looked around and recognized some of the protesters who had been arrested only hours before and had made their way to the dance hall since their release. Many now sat entranced by drugs staring inside themselves too oblivious for the moment to remember or care about the cause which had called them out to rally. He considered what each one might be contemplating then recalled his own earlier baseball reveries and discovered within himself a disenchantment for the images of those same and other heroes whose athletic exploits, womanly beauties or daring soldiery were depicted on television daily and made into the untouchable icons of American culture to which he had always bowed.

As the song's revelation resounded into silence throughout the dance hall the lights flashed on and off to signify the approach of closing time and last call. In the brief clarity which temporary vision accorded him he read graffiti on the wall then heard it echoed aloud by a drunken patron who was unwilling to accept the night's end.

"Fuck off!"

He turned and headed out the door then immediately fell upon another familiar face which he never expected to find in so unfamiliar a place.

"Pete!" he said.

"Joe?" asked his baseball pitcher, "what are you doing here?"

"I come here all the time," he lied, "never seen you here before, though."

"I'm usually in and out," Pete answered in a hurry. "Hey, you know a guy named Henri? He's here all the time too."

"I think I might know him. Long hair always high?" Joe asked describing everyone in the dance hall.

"Yea, that's him, you seen him in there? There's something I need to talk to him about."

"No, man, I didn't see him. I think he was throwing a party at his place."

"I thought he might but I wasn't sure. I figured I'd try here just in case," Pete May tried to disguise his unease and added in a depressed tone, "I guess I'll see you later."

"Hey, man, are you going to Henri's now? 'cos I could really use some downers, right now."

"Uh, yea," Pete said leading him to Coach's car parked across the street, "I didn't know you did downs."

"Not too often, right? Say what'cha doing with Coach this late?" he asked seeing Coach Parker's expression change behind the driver's seat as he approached.

"You know," Pete was cryptic, "working the lumber."

"Huh," replied Joe unimpressed.

They reached the car and Pete sat in the front leaving Joe to invite himself into the back seat.

"Hey, Coach," he said once the door was shut. "Goin' on a downer-run?"

Coach Parker shot Pete a stern look and then turned to Joe in the mirror and said, "You understand Joe that if we take you into our confidence its because we know we can trust you."

"Sure Coach," Joe said flippantly dismissing the implied accusation, "I won't say anything. I'm looking for some downs too."

He pulled out two dollars from his pocket and handed it to him as they drove down the road.

"What? You didn't get any?" Coach asked looking at the money.

"No, Henri wasn't there but Joe thinks he'll be at his place throwing a party," Pete answered. "Isn't that right, Joe?"

"Henri told me himself he was throwing a party, Coach. I just don't know where he lives."

"I know where he lives," Coach asserted while Pete tuned the radio in the awkward silence of the ride that followed summoning Peter, Paul & Mary's Puff the Magic Dragon.

"This is alright," said Pete turning up the volume and then scanning the street that rolled by outside the window.

When the car stopped Pete shut the radio and they all listened for the sound of music coming from the house. Hearing the faint accompanied warbles of lyrical antagonism they looked at each other satisfied that Henri was home throwing a party.

"I'll be right back," Pete said starting to get out and then stopping when he realized Joe was about to follow him in. He said, "Wait here, Joe, he doesn't know I'm coming and he won't like it if I bring someone with me."

"He won't mind," Joe said, "he invited me earlier."

Joe was about to climb out of the vehicle when Coach interrupted him saying, "Stay here, Harmer, we don't want Henri getting mad at Pete."

So ordered, Joe closed his door again and Coach turned up the radio. They sat until Puff had withdrawn into his cave. Remembering the simple melody of the next song he began to sing quietly to himself.

"Trained to live, off nature's land

"Trained in combat, hand to hand

"Men who fight by night and day

"But only …"

Pete's door opened and slammed shut again.

"Well?" Coach asked.

"No," Pete replied in a withdrawn fashion deprived of his pills.

All three remained quiet while they each considered what to do next.

"Say, Coach?"

"What is it? Joe," Coach Parker said driving off again, "you worried about what the scouts would say if they ever figured you were on dope?"

"Not right just now, no. Coach I don't much feel like headin' home tonight," he began to explain, "do you think that maybe I could hang out with you and Pete at your place until morning?"

"What's the matter Joe?" Coach asked with some suspicion.

"I got into a bit of trouble today," he said.

"Oh?" coach looked at him concerned, "what kind of trouble?"

He hesitated for a moment while the others waited for him to reply and then said, "I was at the rally downtown."

"You know the Major teams frown on players who participate in those kinds of rallies, don't you?"

"Yea," Joe said, "well, actually, no. I didn't know but the thought did cross my mind."

"Its not likely anyone will have noticed you were there today but you have to be careful Joe. You could lose your chance to play in a professional league, even if you were only just seen at a riot," Coach said with emphasis. "Besides, what those people do is un-American. What were they up to today? Chanting anti-war slogans? insulting our president?!"

Joe paused as he considered how best to explain and then resolved to say, "I burned my draft-card today."

Coach's foot lifted off the accelerator as he registered what Joe had just said. He had to reflect a moment while trying to pattern a reply in his head that would carry the weight of importance which he placed on the matter. Unable to conjure the wisdom he wished for he simply asked, "Why would you do a thing like that, Joe?"

"Yea, Joe, isn't your brother in Vietnam?" Pete asked.

"I'm not sure why, Coach," he said and then turned to Pete to answer his question, "My brother died on monday."

"Ah, shit Joe, I'm sorry, man. I didn't know."

Joe nodded his head at his friend's condolences.

"So, is it alright if I come over tonight?" he asked Coach again.

"But I don't understand why you would do something that

stupid, Joe. Why would you risk everything you've worked for by setting fire to your draft card? In public!"

"It was just something I had to do."

"Your brother's recent death, the ball scouts and that girl of yours, how are you dealing with things?"

"I don't know but I guess I should get another draft-card since the cops said they're going to ask me for it in about a week. Can I stay with you tonight, Coach, there's a lot I want to get off my mind."

"Sure, Joe, we'll drop Pete off and you and I can," he hesitated and gave Pete a quick look then said, "talk."

"But Coach! What about me?" Pete protested.

"What about you, Pete? I'm driving you home. What more do you want?"

"But I don't want to go home," he pleaded, "maybe Henri'll have some downs in a couple of hours."

"We ain't gonna work the lumber tonight, Pete," Coach replied, "no need for you to get upset. Joe just needs to talk and get things off his mind. That's all."

They pulled up to Pete's house and he reluctantly got out of the car and gave Joe the front seat. Without looking to Pete, Joe slammed the door shut and Coach slapped Joe's thigh then pushed the stick into gear.

Chapter 10

"Local Youths Burn Draft Cards"

LIGHT SHONE THROUGH THE LIVING room window when Joe woke up prostrate on the couch. The television was still on and empty beer cans littered the floor around the easy-chair where Coach had passed out loitering in an open bathrobe flaunting his raggedy underwear and stale t-shirt from the night before. Sports pages lay strewn about the coffee-table reporting baseball news from every league in the country and a crumbling copy of the year's *Sports Illustrated : Scouting Reports* sat beneath an open jar of vaseline next to a stiff new undersized glove, greased, balled and bound ready to be broken in.

Joe dislodged himself from the loose covers and dropped his feet to the floor recognizing the sound of a doorbell followed by a knock.

"Coach Parker," whispered a small boy through the mail slot.

He dressed and tied his boots while waiting to see if the drunk and dormant tot-tutor would wake up and get the door. By the time the boy had bustled off his boots were tied and he was counting the buttons missing from his shirt. Making certain he had left nothing behind he peered through the blinds to be certain there was no ambush waiting for him outside then he headed for the door. The newspaper boy who had just made his round to Coach's house left a rolled copy of saturday's Herald on the door-step. He stooped to pick up the print-for-profit purveyor of public opinion and had a look at the front cover uncertain if a draft-card burning rally was front page news and found that the black and white still photo of himself standing next to a burning trashcan on the front cover beneath the headline "Local Youths Burn Draft Cards" gave evidence that it was.

He read the first few lines and was content that the article's vitriolic jingoist ring would sway social sympathies against him. Charged by what he had read he stuffed the paper into the letter box and sauntered along the footpath and onto the sidewalk strolling past the early morning traffic. Confident of his moral mandate Joe's thoughts distracted him as he paraded on towards his family's home. The morning chill lifted as he walked the rest of the way certain that even though he knew his mission was a noble one his parents could not understand and their ignorance would cause them grief for as long as he was underground.

The elderly neighbor who had spent afternoons with him playing catch between their lawns stood on his steps now and greeted Joe's arrival with a sad shake of his head, a downcast disbelieving stare and a final turn of his shoulder while clutching the Herald in his hand. Understanding the old man's disappointment but unable to explain the nobility of his actions he winced away the hurt he felt from this aging friend's offense. His boots made dewy depressions on his family lawn and in a moment he could hear the screeching screen porch door as he entered the house.

"Joe?" his mother launched herself out of her chair to greet him. "Tell me it was a mistake, please son, tell me you didn't do it."

Joe looked at the tears that streaked down her face then let her take hold of him while he prepared to ease the confirmation that would destroy his parents despite his best intentions, "It's alright, mom, I did it for a good reason."

"What reason could there possibly be?" she asked sinking back into her seat crushed with disappointment.

His father sat at the kitchen table next to them and Joe could see the blood rising into his face, neck and shoulders, as the ex-marine held back the anger that convulsed and brimmed in him. Tension wrung Mr.Harmer's nerves and his war worn wits threatened to march him into madness.

"I had to, mom, trust me. I just can't explain," Joe pleaded in a failed attempt to follow through with the explanation he had planned.

"What could you possibly be thinking, Joe?" Mrs.Harmer cried looking at him with a shamed faced. "Do you know what the neighbors are saying? Joe! What are you on about?"

He looked at her and understood the sting she suffered. He knew that any news that he had joined the marines so soon after Michael's death would have aggravated her grief but seeing the ignoble image of her only living son plastered onto the front page of the local newspaper inciting everyone she knew to convict him as the latest local patriotic execrant seemed a worse calamity than if he had been lost in the jungles of Vietnam.

"I can't say, mom, just trust me."

He turned away from her and headed for the stairs.

"Don't turn your back on your mother!" bellowed Mr.Harmer as he stood up to his full height. "You hear me, Joe! Come back here and explain to her why you would shame this family!"

Joe froze in his steps and considered rethinking his original plan then turned around and approached the table again. His mother pulled him to his seat before Mr.Harmer exploded and urged them both to sit down.

As the three regained their seats Mrs.Harmer's friend came to the door, "Vicky? Is everything alright?"

Still distraught but brave enough to recover before her friend's appearance, Mrs.Harmer answered from where she sat shouting towards the door as calmly as should could desiring not to show herself, "Yes, Lisa. Thanks again. We'll talk later."

Mrs. Sommers hovered by the door trying to hear what she had been sent to report and finally accepted her dismissal, "Ok. I'll come by later."

"Alright," Mrs.Harmer tried to sound pleased, "see you later."

The three remained silent as they listened to Mrs.Sommers exercise the tact of stealth outside until Mr.Harmer spoke up again.

"Joe, you can't expect your mother and I to just accept that you could think it right to go and do something as stupid as burn your G-D draft-card!" he said staring down his son from across the table and pushing the newspaper at him.

"There's more to what you see!" Joe tried to sound reasonable but realized it was futile to argue.

"Joe, please," his mother said still on the verge of tears, "what were you thinking?"

She spotted the remains of dark ink on his hands and grabbed his wrists to turn them then thrust them over the table to show his father.

"So its true! You did get arrested," his father growled, "do you know how that will look on your military record if you get drafted? It won't matter if you graduate from M.I.T. anymore because now you'll have a criminal record and no one will ever give you a job. You stay up all night, get into fights and come home boozed up scaring your mother half to death in the process. That's two nights in a row now that you don't come home like you've always done. I didn't want to believe it when Mrs.Blaise called to tell your mother that Mr.Blaise won't let you see Jennifer anymore on account of you getting her arrested! Think of those around you, Joe! We've all been hurt by your brother's passing but that don't give you no right to make more hurt for your mother."

"Joe," Mrs.Harmer began, "tell me you don't have a criminal record. Tell me you're not going to jail!"

"No, no, Vicky," said Mr.harmer, "and there ain't no point in Joe going to school either, no how. The only way he can make up for what he's done is by heading straight to the recruitment office and proving himself a Harmer! No judge will even fine him for burning his G-D draft-card once he shows up at court wearing his Blue Dress uniform."

Mrs.Harmer knew she couldn't change her husband's mind and worried that she might lose her second son like she had the first. Trying to understand the end of her world she anxiously looked to Joe for an explanation.

"I won't go to jail for burning my draft-card, dad," Joe

explained mechanically and with as little emotion as he allowed to escape, "because I didn't burn my draft-card."

Relieved but aghast to hear this they were left stunned in confusion.

"But if you didn't burn your draft-card, Joe, what did you burn?" his father asked hoping there was a positive resolution to their problem.

"Mom," Joe began again seeing the expectation in their eyes, "dad. Yesterday, after we got news that Michael had died, I walked Jennifer home and we talked."

"Yes?" Mrs.Harmer reached out to hold his hand as he spoke, "and…"

His father sat dumbfound at the possible endings which this tale could take and wondered where he would carry it.

"and," Joe continued, "after I dropped her off I walked around by myself a while and I realized that I had to decide what I was going to do with myself. My future. You're right about baseball. I shouldn't waste my time there when I've got a chance to go to school. but I could do both."

He stopped there in his explanation and let his parents digest that thought for a moment. It was clear to Joe that his father now weighed the idea of his son in colored-pajamas dancing in the dirt for money playing baseball against the alternative of carting him off to incarceration for dodging the draft, but nothing could excuse the shame of seeing a picture of him at a protest rally on the front page of the Herald.

"However," Joe took some effort to deliver himself as he continued to speak, "last night I decided I would do you both proud and enlisted in the U.S. Marine Corps."

Mr.Harmer was thrown back in his chair by this revelation

while Mrs.Harmer clutched Joe's hand wondering why he would say this.

"But if you've already joined why did you go to the rally and say what the Herald reports," his mother looked at him sensing he was lying.

They waited for an answer beyond Mr.Harmer's patience and he finally demanded to know, "well?!? What happened? Why did you go to the rally?"

"Because," he began again with a creak in his voice fearing their worst reaction, "because when I spoke to the officers at the MEPS..."

He swallowed hard and made an audible sound which distracted them all and he was promptly urged on by his mother, "well? You went to be processed and...? What did they say?"

"Yesterday," he tried once more embarrassed to tell them what he had to say, "when I was at the protest rally, I didn't burn my draft-card, dad. I burned my Class 4-F selective service card."

"What?!" Mr.Harmer jumped to his feet, "Joe! You aren't 4-F! No son of mine is a goddamn 4-F! How could they possibly classify you a 4-F? Did you tell them you were accepted at M.I.T.?!"

"Yea, dad," Joe apologized fearfully stepping away from him as his father rounded the table and towered over him outraged, "I told them."

Vainly Mrs.Harmer tried to intercede but was kept to the side and ignored.

"Did you tell them the baseball league fancies you playing for their team?"

"Yea, dad," Joe explained, "they know that. It wasn't a matter of health."

"Well, it couldn't be a mental issue, dear," said his mother hoping her tone would ease her husband's already overly-taut nerves.

"No, no," Joe agreed, "its not a mental issue either. I'm fully competent in both regards. Its just that…"

Mr.Harmer considered the ways a candidate could be rejected and slouched his head in shame.

"What is it," asked Mrs.Harmer.

"Get out, boy," said the humiliated veteran, "get the hell out of my house. And don't you come back!"

Chapter 11

YOU'RE WITH ME

"CHARLES!" SAID A SHOCKED MRS.HARMER, "you can't!"

"Get out of my house, boy," Joe's father repeated lifting his head with black unseeing eyes that stared through him.

"Come along, Joe," whispered his mother leading him to the door, "Your father will change his mind. Come back in an hour when he'll be at the foundry. He's upset for now, but he doesn't mean it. Really he doesn't."

"I know, mom," Joe said giving her a parting hug on the top step, "I know."

She shoved him off fearing Mr.Harmer may lose his patience and Joe was away marching alone beneath the loathing looks of neighbors who, though having known him his entire life, could now only see what they had never imagined. Superimposed over years of love and admiration for a boy they thought they knew so well was a single image that would forever reflect their view of him in the harsh black and white tones that only a public medium can provide. He felt the weight of their stares and only by recalling the mandate which had given him purpose could he raise his head in defiance of their anger. Though he soon put his family home behind him, and despite being able to let the street sign on the corner pass by him without looking back, he was certain that it would be some time before he could forget the emotions of that day.

Digging in his pockets he found the remnants of a small lump of bills and the rough Zippo he had stolen from his father's sock drawer the previous day. His hand gripped the sturdy pocket-knife Michael gave him years before, a hand-me-down he inherited at the advent of his brother's puberty when the elder sibling discovered sylph nymphs, gangly girls and slender lasses. With little but his boots to carry him along he made his way to Jennifer's house unsure whether habit or desire had drawn him there but once he had reached the deserted driveway determined to see her he purposefully approached the house from the side. Her parents would not be pleased to see him and although Mr. Blaise was sure to be away, the sound of the vacuum cleaner in the basement near the front of the house suggested that Mrs. Blaise was not.

Though he couldn't be certain Jennifer would be home, or predict how she might greet him, he slipped beneath the opened window and into the yard then climbed onto the rear porch noting the charcoal ash in the barbecue by the door had been replaced by thin black sheets of cinder. Careful not to alert Mrs. Blaise of his intrusion or arrival, he carefully opened the patio door and entered the house he knew as well as his own then trod his way to Jennifer's bedroom and entered without knocking hoping to find an accomplice there but discovered that his fetching vestal was absent. The walls of her room, normally concealed behind newspaper clippings and a portrait of Margaret Mead, were censured to bare simplicity. Pallid pine stared at him as he wrestled with the lifeless face of stained wood wondering how much trouble her arrest could have caused her as he gently pushed the door shut and sealed himself inside the aseptic cell. Stepping further into the room for a more thorough examination revealed a clean uncluttered desk where a sentient mess of loose notes, scribblings and journals filled with Jennifer's neat scrawl had once taken residence.

Hoping to find some of her compositions concealed inside a drawer he searched those and uncovered nothing but bits of crayon and a few morsels of shredded paper, remains left behind by the vulgar hands that had taken everything else away. He stood worried for a moment wondering once again just how angry her parents could be and, finding himself without the paper on which he had intended to write her a note, he began to make a dumb draft of what he would have said as he squat down onto the rug at the foot of Jennifer's bed. The fire he had set, since fueled by Jennifer's arrest, kindled a feud he had never expected.

Only now realizing how drastic an impact so simple an act of rebellion, or even the appearance of rebellion, could have on his life and the lives of those around him Joe concluded that his father would eternally feel the stinging shame of knowing his son had been publicly branded a coward, while holding silent and keeping to himself the repugnant belief that he could have sired and raised a boy deemed morally unfit for military service. Joe understood that the reflection he saw in the tears streaking down his mother's cheeks was not his own but one tainted by the necessities which the mission he had accepted for himself imposed. And at this moment, on the floor alone in Jennifer's room, he stared blankly at the bare pine walls and wondered just how dearly those he loved would have to pay for his good intentions and how much he himself would have to sacrifice.

The vacuum cleaner had been silent for some time already before he heard the door open behind him and alarm him to his feet.

"Joe?" Jennifer asked in a whisper while closing the door, "what are you doing here?"

She waited half a pause for an answer and then peered out through the door to see if anyone was behind her and then shut it closed once more.

"Jennifer," he said beguiled to see her, "what happened?"

She urged him towards the window, opened it and threw her head outside to scout the lawn then pulled herself in again in a near panic and said, "You have to go! Quickly. She'll see you."

Joe stood there an instant trying to apologize, "I'm sorry, Jennifer. Where are your articles? What happened to your writing? the portrait?"

Seeing that he wasn't ready to leave without an answer she forfeited an explanation, "my parents are real, right mad, Joe. If it weren't for Mr. Ricci getting the police to drop the charges I don't know what they would have done. I'm grounded so I can't go to work anymore and they're talking about not letting me go to college. They mustn't see you here. You wouldn't believe the things they said about you! I'm sorry, Joe, but they just can't find you here."

"But Jennifer, I came to tell you…"

A knock on the door behind her heightened her alarm and the tension in her voice betrayed her anxiety.

"It's ok, mom, I'll be right there."

The door opened and Joe stood guilty in the eyes of her mother.

"Joe Harmer! Haven't you done enough?"

"Please, let me explain," he begged.

"There's nothing to explain," she replied, "get out of here before I call the police."

"But Mrs.Blaise, please," he tried again.

"Get out!" she shouted and threatened to hit him with her broom.

Seeing her make a wide step to the side to let him pass, Joe fled the room.

"We'll discuss this with your father when he comes home," Jennifer's mother uttered menacingly.

Promising to himself that he would return once he had completed his task he leaped out the front door with adrenaline beating his chest and setting a pace akin to a sprint in his disheveled retreat only slowing to a quick walk when he reached the next corner. There he redirected his distraught strides towards the Pleasant Hill bus depot trying to focus on what he could still control rather than distract himself with wasted worries over the woes of those he loved and hurt, and whom he now knew he would have to leave behind despite the great concern he held for them.

With the bus depot still several blocks away he walked struggling with thoughts that ranged from how he would miss his Jennifer and how little he could do to ease his mother's pain. The haunting sight of his father's face, twisted with torment, fraught and fatigued by age, anger and shame, was etched in his head to remind him of the fire he had set. The dreams of the baseball career he had thrown away, the meditative meanderings along M.I.T.'s riverside campus that he had rejected and the quiet life in Pleasant Hill with Jennifer which he destroyed, were all overshadowed by ruminations of the ROTC training he could have elected for himself had he but only refused the offer he received the night he went to the recruitment office rather than accept class 4-F papers along with the ignominy they brought him in exchange for his service.

He found himself standing in line to buy tickets at the inter-state counter of the town bus depot. Few people recognized him and those that did either had not seen the morning's Herald, didn't care what he had done, or simply chose to ignore him rather than risk associating with so coarse a character. When his turn at the wicket arrived he heard himself mechanically purchase a ticket to Philadelphia and was not asked for I.D. The three hour ride which he planned to catch was there waiting to depart in twenty minutes, leaving him little time to dawdle, shop or dine. A line had already formed in front of his gate and so he soon found a place at the end of it. He watched the bus driver greet his passengers with a hole punch as they shuffled along and boarded with tickets in their pockets and baggages in their hands. When he reached the front of the line he climbed the steps unimpeded by any luggage, then marched to the back of the bus confident he would soon escape Pleasant Hill, though he knew his worries would not be quelled by his leaving. Following in after him were several couples and an elderly woman who struggled with a large bag and was given some assistance by a young girl still in her teen-aged years.

Behind them, and arriving last only seconds before the doors were shut for the trip, was an unshaven and dirty rough-hand. A biker type by appearance with shoulder-length unwashed hair and filth-stained leather vest over a muddy blood-encrusted t-shirt. He looked out of place, bowed over and confined inside the bus, making his fellow travelers wince at the sight of him as he passed the empty seats and each one feared he might choose to sit down beside them.

The back of the bus seemed the only reasonable place for him to sit so Joe was not surprised to see himself joined by so memorable a character as this one.

"Is this seat taken?" he asked in a scratchy but sober voice.

"No," Joe said amiably, "go ahead."

His travel companion sat down beside him and extended a hand.

"Frank," he said, "Frank Shade."

Joe took his hand glad to make contact.

"Joe," he replied, "Joe Harmer."

"You ever been to Philli before, Joe?"

"No, sir," he reported.

The bus closed its doors and slowly reared out of the depot then started on its way.

Shade leaned over in his chair and looked down the aisle before saying in a quiet tone certain no one else would hear, "I knows what you done, Joe. And I'm right kind to one as such as you. And you and I both know that you ain't got no one and nowhere in Philli. And the training you might've got from some of 'em elsewhere? Well, I'm the one that gives it to you, now. So you don't gotta worry about none and all that 'cos now you're with me."

Chapter 12
BONNY RIDE

"YOU GOT ANY LUGGAGE?" SHADE asked as they stepped off the bus.

"No," Joe's reply concealed little of his anxiety.

"Then we won't have to hang out here. Come on."

Joe followed after him looking around at the strange buildings and crowds of people in the city while trying to keep up with the hurried pace Shade maintained despite the heat. Passing several historic sites which a less harried Joe Harmer might have enjoyed more than a brief perusal, they made their way along the busy sidewalks of downtown Philadelphia into a slightly less densely quartered area and marched on foot a ways further until they reached the back lot of a motorcycle repair shop.

"Hi Frank," said the gear-head squatting next to his craft, "bring us a new monkey?"

"Not this time, Mitch," Shade answered with a friendly wave.

"What was that about?" asked Joe when they'd entered into the shop's back door.

"Never mind, you ride?"

"Motorcycle? Once or twice."

They passed a dozen used bikes and a row of wooden shelves filled with new and used parts along their way into the retail area of the shop where the chromed steeds were corralled on display.

"Mike, I got a cousin I want you to meet," Shade said to the clerk as a way of introduction. "This is Joe Harmer. He'll be running errands for me at the club out west. I want you to hook him up with a ride."

"Cousin, huh," the old retired gray-haired Ranger wiped some oil from his rag onto his hand and looked at Joe, "and he wants a bike, does he. He ride much?"

"Police impounded his CB before he jumped bail," explained Shade loud enough for the other customers to hear him, "you got somethin'? It doesn't have to be pretty."

"CB, huh," Mike stuffed a corner of the rag into the pocket of his overalls and led them to the back, "I don't keep CBs here, nor work on them. Don't much care for 'em. But I've got a Bonneville."

Joe looked the bikes over trying to guess which one was the Bonneville until the shop's owner straddled a sharp looking one with a blue tank and stood it up. Bouncing on the seat to test its springs the cog tinker wheeled the English Bonny out into the yard and pressed the ignition bringing it to life.

"What d'ya think?" he asked over the din of the engine.

Without considering Joe's opinion, Shade replied, "That'll be fine. He'll need some gear."

"Vest? gloves?" asked Mike cutting the engine, "what does he need?"

Shade looked Joe over and said, "Just a good vest. You sure

that bike's alright? My cousin's not gonna find his brake-line's drained or the clutch don't work, will he?"

Mike asked half serious and taking on an offended air as they headed back inside, "Frank, have you ever had any problems with my bikes?"

"There's bound to be a first," Shade laughed pleased to conclude this business then turning to Joe he said, "Come on."

They followed the piston peddler back inside.

"When d'ya get these?" Shade asked taking up a helmet.

"Ordered them last week," Mike said derisively, "my supplier says they'll be mandatory soon."

"Like hell!" Shade shook his head. "Where'd he hear that?"

"Its in the news, Frank," Mike assured him, "Federal this and state that about some highway funding or something, its always about money. Pennsylvania's likely to make it a law that sez no one can ride without one!"

Shade made a face, "you gotta be kiddin?!?"

"Johnson's Federal Funding of State highway reconstruction is contingent on each state's enactment of mandatory helmet use," Joe announced glad to have something to say.

"Well fancy him!" Mike said sounding genuinely offended this time, "next he'll tell us what Bill Scranton has a mind to."

"Governor Scranton is unlikely to find opposition in the state legislative assembly when a statute is finally drafted and put forward since any member of the assembly who tries to oppose it would …"

"When Mike says to 'shut up', you shut up!" said Shade cutting Joe short in a harsh rebuking tone.

"But he just said…"

"Shut up," Shade glared down at Joe and handed him a leather vest, "put this on."

The greasy geezer glared at Joe until he turned away giving Shade and he the opportunity to grin and laugh at him while he donned the vest he was given.

The old man nodded at his friend then gruffed them off, "the bonny's gonna need an oil change when you get to Columbus or it won't make it all the way to the west coast."

"We'll stop by Tommy's in Wheeling," Shade assured him marching Joe towards the back.

He pushed his Harley Davidson Panhead out from the crowd of iron that remained by the door until its chrome glittered in the sunshine next to Joe's Bonneville.

"We're gonna drive out a ways and have a talk," Shade continued to glare at Joe menacingly, "you stay behind me."

"Sure," Joe shouted over the purr of his engine as he toyed with the clutch.

Shade turned the Harley's ignition key, jumped down on the starter pedal and woke up the beast. Cranking the throttle and making it roar, the engine was shaking beneath him when he looked up and found that Joe had beaten him to the gate on his Bonneville. Jumping off the Harley and leaving it idly humming on its stand Shade leaped the four paces after Joe, who sat stupid and distracted by the bike's gauges, and grabbed the Bonneville's clutch with his left hand, kicked the stand down using his opposite foot and tossed Joe to the dirt in one practiced and experienced throw. After toeing the gears into neutral and releasing the clutch he turned to his subordinate who was sprawled on the ground covered in dirt and struck him with a knee to the head.

Thrown onto his back Joe was unsure what to do next when Shade picked him up by the leather handles he'd wrapped him in and hoarsely whispered his first command, "fight!"

Given his instructions Joe began swinging wildly knocking Shade back with a surprising haymaker as Mitch and Mike, along with nearby pedestrians who caught the show, stopped what they were doing and watched the brawl. Joe charged Shade with rabid jabs, blindly bashing and punching. Though surprising his antagonist with the ferocity of his attack he failed to connect against the more experienced fighter who effortlessly ducked, dodged and deflected each strike while taking every opportunity to counter from a choice of weapons held in the arsenal of his empty hands. Directing open hand or fist, knee or elbow at his opponent in timely attacks that struck with violent effect, Shade managed the combat long enough for Joe to put out his heart then swept him to the dirt and lectured him on the proper etiquette of a motorcycle rally.

"You stay BEHIND me!" he said with his knee on Joe's chest, "don't make me tell you again."

He threw him to his feet and measured the fight left in his eyes while Joe stared up at him with an undaunted menacing glare.

"Good," said Shade throwing his arm around the boy's shoulder and leading him to the Bonneville, "now get on your ride."

Joe tottered towards his Bonny, leaned on its handles for support as he caught his breath and was in gear wiping blood from his mouth with the shoulder of his sleeve staying in Shade's rear-view mirror while a slow breeze cooled the bruises on his face. He could feel his left eye slowly swelling shut as he spat out the taste of blood lingering around his split lip. The streets turned to roads and the roads turned to highways and Joe's fears dissolved behind him, as the two knights of the iron steeds rumbled over the dusty pavement.

They prepared to arrest themselves when Shade turned off the highway and into a rest-area where he led his vassal near the main building, parked his bike then marched off towards the restrooms where he ordered Joe to clean up. Emerging from the loo, with the dirt on his face smeared into two mud stains that streaked down the sides of his neck, Joe met Shade standing at the Cafeteria counter.

"Coffee and some fries," he ordered, "you want anything?"

"Pop?" Joe asked uncertain.

"Anything else?"

"No," he replied.

His appearance, though cleaner since his visit to the rest rooms, distressed the waitress who was in the habit of serving long haul truckers and vacationing families.

"And a pop for my friend."

After paying for their refreshments Shade guided Joe to an isolated table for a short briefing.

"Have some fries?" he said squirting a generous spread of ketchup on them.

"Sure," Joe took a swig of his pop and pulled a long fried potato from the plate.

Shade let him eat the plate while he talked, "Yer gonna help me at my road-house. A lot of bikers hangout there so the new badges on your face'll help you get along. Most of the crowd just like to party and fuck off but some of 'em have business to run so we gotta watch 'em and interfere without really interfering. You got a few patched one-percenters who drop by on occasion but for the most part the war goes on elsewhere without us meddling in it."

"The war?"

"Yea, the bikers war with each other and though the Sickos have settled into the Gas Light they're too small to object if one of the bigger clubs were to move in. I keep an eye on the local-politics 'cos its my business but they're not the dogs we're after." Shade sipped his steaming coffee, "Heroin is the big fish. We sell the green and its all local weed but the H comes from all over the place. And I don't like seeing money going somewheres I don't know where its goin'. That means we find the leak and plug it."

Joe munched on the fries thoughtfully while Shade pulled out a smoke.

"You got a light?"

Mechanically drawing his father's Zippo out of his pocket Joe placed it on the table and watched Shade light his cigarette then retrieved the old keepsake.

"The crank-run business you told me about on the bus is small time but I'll make sure he's looked after. As for your coach, his kind shifts around when they're discovered but I'll make sure the word gets to the right people, they'll know what to do with 'em."

An elderly tourist on his way to a far table gave them both a wary look and passed by them along his way prompting Shade to sip his coffee and think of what else there was left to say.

"I run the Gas-Light myself and the staff'll think you're my cousin. And it don't matter if they'd never heard of ya 'cos that's none of their business no how. The staff are all unaffiliated nobodies doing their 9 to 5 at a road-house so you don't talk to them about nothin' but the price of whiskey and beer. I'll hook you up with all the weed you need to sell and make contacts, and get drunk, and we'll have our regular man-to-mans to get you goin'," he started getting up and Joe followed him towards the door, "you ever handle a gun?"

"Once or twice," Joe lied.

"I figured," Shade understood, "you probably read Shakespeare! I've a range out on the farm by the road-house you'll get a look at. Got a punching bag too and he's taken a kind beatin' already but he's never let me down, that's why I call 'em *Job*," he smiled. "First thing, when we get to Frisco, you're gonna teach Job a right lesson. There'll be books an' lernin' an all that but it won't be much matter to you."

With nothing more needing to be said they gulped down their drinks and found their bikes again. Shade kicked his Harley to life then added, "And if anybody asks about you and me bein' cousins, you just tell'em to fuck off and go about your business."

Chapter 13

GAS LIGHT

THE FAINT JINGLE BOUNCING OUT of a Mustang's eight-track in the lane beside him filtered its way into the cab of Shade's beat-down pickup as Joe sat behind the wheel waiting for the traffic light to change its hue. The simple world in which the children of the Beach Boys ballad abided for a chance to "hold each other close the whole night through" triggered an emotion in him he didn't recognize until he reached the corner and made a right turn while the song was carried off straight ahead fading as it went.

"Oh Wouldn't it be nice…"

He missed Jennifer. He had never missed her before. And aside from his brother Michael, he had never missed anyone else either.

He was running late on an errand to pick up groceries for the Gas Light's 'Continental Breakfast'. It was a good thing that their guests rarely rose before noon, he thought, or he would have to worry about being late though it wasn't likely that anyone would miss the stale buns, toast and dried out fruit that was the normal fare which fueled them before the day's debauchery began. He turned into the grocer's lot and stalled the truck in the first available parking spot then headed inside not bothering to lock the doors or close the windows. Always in a hurry since they first arrived in California, he pressed the pace and hastened himself through to the bakery where he grabbed some day-old French-loaves sitting in a display stand then dashed down the dairy aisle and picked two bricks of cheeses and a pound of butter.

As he held these intended purchases precariously balanced in his left arm while groping for not over-riped tomatoes, and wishing he had taken a shopping basket at the door, he thought he caught sight of his mother near the cash register, despite the three thousand mile distance between them. It worried him that she would be hurt if she saw her son so disheveled, and chose to inspect himself in the mirror that hung behind the vegetable stall rather than face the strange woman. As he stared back at that image he saw the unshaved sideburns that had comfortably taken root on his cheeks framing the new scars which life as a biker road-house go'fer had given him. Almost dropping one of the cheese bricks out from under his arm as he did, and while watching the woman in the familiar blouse out of the corner of his eye disappear from the store, he managed to bag four tomatoes without damaging them too badly. Crumpling the paper bag to make it fit his grip, Joe tried to recall the last time he had bathed and, having no exact memory of doing so recently, decided to add that task to his list of chores, possibly for sometime next week, or to use the shammy on himself at least once the next time Shade ordered him to clean his Harley.

Still juggling dairy bricks with dough sticks he skipped past the feminine hygiene section without letting his eyes stray from the ceiling until he found the *Old Spice* deodorants he was looking for then winced when, in his haste, he slapped his tender tomatoes against the shelving trying to grab the bottled bouquet causing the brown bag to bleed through a tear. Looking both ways to be certain no one was watching, he dropped the squashed nosh to the floor and kicked it under the display shelf then headed towards the check out aisle. The cashier, who was now used to seeing him almost habitually, no longer worried for her till when he approached as she once had and reluctantly grew accustomed to his profane appearance and indifferent demeanor.

"Hiya, Ruth," he said reading the name tag pinned to her chest in a friendlier tone than their transaction warranted, "what do I owe you today?"

Beyond a reserved smile in acknowledgment to his greeting the cashier ignored him and punched up his purchases then said, "that comes to $4.78."

Paying her what she asked, he got his change then turned and noticed that a dimpled wrapper had rushed over to bag his groceries.

"Help you to your car, sir?" asked the juvenile victuals valet.

"Sure," Joe replied calculating in his head what he still had in stock.

Once outside, his aproned customer whispered, "Joe, man, I need a score."

Certain this would happen, Joe nodded with a broad grin and opened the passenger side door so that the bag boy could put his groceries on the seat. Already an expert at this transaction, he withdrew the product from one of his deep pockets and made the exchange, handing him the pay-packet envelope of pressed, wet, smelly pot and stashing the two one dollar bills he got in exchange while thanking him for carrying his bags to the truck.

Behind the wheel once more he stabbed the ignition with his keys. The truck whined and grunted then whirled itself to life again and he turned into the flowing traffic. Having no hardware needs or other liquor errands to run in town for the day he turned onto the deserted rural road between himself and the Gas Light Hotel. Within a few minutes of hearing the wind whistling through his opened window he could see the faded unlit placard advertising the hotel's vacancy and the not uncommon sight of a police cruiser parked outside. He pulled up beside it wondering what the trouble was today then grabbed the bags of groceries and walked past the bar's entrance heading towards the hotel's front office where he expected to find Bailey, their timorous attendant.

"And you have no idea where he might have gone to?" asked the police officer standing at the desk.

"No, no, sir," conceded the clerk while shaking his head and flipping the pages of the registry. "Says here, he showed up but three days ago and I don't recall ever seeing the gentleman as I only work here during the day and the registry says he arrived late in the evening."

"Can you show me his room?"

"Well, now, I don't know if Mr. Shade would approve," Bailey's once pristine white shirt began to gather sweat as he nervously asserted the hotel's policy to the police. "Let me see if I can fetch him."

Joe carried the groceries through the office towards the stairs leading to the rooms and the bar beyond them.

"Afternoon," he said to the cop who tipped his hat in greeting.

He made it to the bar without dropping anything and was accosted near the door.

"Have you seen Frank?"

It was the the hotel's latest asset, Julia, who's job it was to encourage the sale of alcohol and see that the guests found their way to their rooms.

"No, I just got here. Why?"

He placed the bags on the bar then took hold of the back of her arm and ushered her to the side and spoke in the suggestion of a whisper, "what's going on?"

Julia's bright red toreador pants molded themselves around her slender legs which appeared longer by the illusion her tarnished red heels created. The white beer stained buttoned down top she wore to cover her chest was tied about her waist revealing a bra that struggled from fatigue.

"Frank brought a guest to my room last night," she said.

He waited for her to finish then asked, "so?!?"

"So," she continued, "the guy's still there."

Shade's voice reached them from the office.

"We're always willing to cooperate with the police," he said, "Bailey fetch the keys."

"Yes, sir, Mr.Shade."

The sound of keys slipping off a hook and the closing of a cabinet was followed by a cluster of footfalls heading towards the stairs.

"A mess in the hallway?" Joe asked hushing his voice.

"No, but we'll need the blood and puke crew in my room," she explained.

"Right," he said while thinking then added, "go back

upstairs and keep things quiet. I'll bring up the crew when the pig leaves."

He held her arm until she nodded her compliance then watched her go. The bar was empty and he wondered where the waitress was then looked at the time and realized neither girls had started their shift yet. Wondering if he might still find the maid somewhere in the building he went to the office and inquired.

"Hey, Bailey?"

"Yea, Joe," the agitated hotel clerk sat up unsure whether or not he should stand for a fellow subordinate then found himself straightened and alert, "what is it? Have the police found anything?"

"No, no," Joe replied easing Bailey who was always quick to alarm, "have you seen Jessica?"

"Mrs. Haile went home, Joe. Mr. Haile was here just a short while ago to pick her up," catching Joe's disappointment he added, "Vera called to say she was late coming back from New York but that Mattie would be here."

"Neither's shown up yet?"

"I don't right know, Joe, but if Vera said that Mattie was taking her shift then Mattie…"

"Never mind, Bailey," he interrupted rudely and turned towards the bar again where he spotted Vera as soon as he walked in. "Hi!"

"Hi, Joe," replied the buxom blond with the short curly hair.

She turned her ass towards him and deliberately jut out her butt while pulling down her skirt and looking for a reaction through the mirror.

"I thought you were gonna be late?"

"Huh?" she asked pursing her lips to paint them red.

"Bailey," he said as explanation and pointing over his shoulder with his thumb.

"Oh, that," she faced him again and hopped to jiggle her breasts pretending she was still fixing her dress, "I met a Broadway producer who asked me to read for him but it didn't pan out."

She grabbed the bag of groceries from the counter and began unlocking the refrigerators.

"What's with the cops?" she asked placing the deodorant and bricks of cheese to one side then taking the bread and butter to the breakfast table.

He muttered an uncertain, "dunno," as he was walking away.

"We need more beer from downstairs!" she shouted after him while standing in front of the walk-in.

"Yea, yea," he waved her off and went upstairs just as Frank was escorting the policeman down again.

"And you don't know where he might have gone to?"

"I'm sorry, officer. It was a crowded night last night and I'd never seen this guest until day before last. Stayed one night, s'far as I know."

"Alright," said the policeman, "be sure to let the department know if you hear anything."

"Will do, boss," Shade replied with confidence. "As soon as I hear anything I'll be on the phone right away."

The patrolman sauntered over to his car, took his hat off before getting inside and drove off.

"Joe!"

"Yea, Frank."

"Bring the crew to Julia's room. We've got a bit of a mess."

Shade stomped up the stairs while Joe headed to the backroom.

"Bit of a mess," Vera chuckled, "wonder what that's about."

"You got breakfast covered?" Joe asked.

"Sure," she soothed cutting the French loaf, "don't worry about a thing."

Joe grabbed his bucket, mop and shovel from the back room then hurried upstairs.

"Its what Sonny said?" Joe heard Julia asking when he reached her locked room.

He lightly tapped on the door with the clean end of the shovel.

"Who is it?"

"Frank," he said, "its Joe."

"You bring the crew?"

Joe looked down at the mop and broom in his hands and confirmed that he had, "yea."

The door swung open and was shut and latched again as soon as he had crossed its frame.

"Where's the mess?" he asked and the nod of Shade's chin indicated the toilet.

A streak of blood on the floor seeped out from the bathroom where a man knelt with his head in the bowl and his hands cuffed around it as if he were hugging the porcelain seat.

Grabbing him by the hair to have a look at his swollen battered face, Joe said, "bet there's some place you'd rather be!"

Chapter 14
THE OUTHOUSE

"WE'RE GONNA MOVE HIM TO the Outhouse," Shade commanded. "Help me untie him."

"Why didn't you just bring him there last night?"

"Not now, Joe," Shade's curt reply hushed his crew man.

Trying not to get too much gore on himself, Shade reached behind the bloody bog and untied a near wrist from its shackle then dumped his unconscious captive into the tub.

"Joe!" Shade shouted forgetting he was standing next to him, "fetch the canvas tent in the shed."

"You want the ropes, spikes and poles?"

"No, just the canvas," Shade explained, "we're gonna wrap him in it before we take him outside."

"Right," Joe blurted bustling to the door.

He stepped into the hallway and heard the latch behind him then headed down the stairs and decided to look in on Bailey at the front desk to make sure everything there was still quiet. The sunlight streamed in through the open window and a light breeze whistled through. The radio was on and their coy clerk stood stooped over it attentive to what sounded like the farm report.

Assured that all was well there he left by the front door and rounded the building. Reaching for the right key on his ring, he opened the shed's lock once he'd crossed the hotel's parking lot. Shade's camping gear in hand he grabbed the canvas tent from the pack, relatched the lock, and headed back inside where he found Bailey taking notes at his desk while still listening to the farm news.

Puzzled by this he stopped and asked, "you intend on buying a farm, Bailey?"

"huh?" hushed the homesteader, "ah, nah, Joe. My girl Jenna says her pa thinks I oughta learn the price of beans before we settle."

"right," Joe wondered and wandered off.

"Cheddar!?" he heard a rough voice berate from the bar, "what?! no Gouda?"

"oh, no," he muttered to himself and lunged into the lounge, "Vera!"

"I don't know, Kenny," the rattled waitress apologized to the old biker who was slapping slabs of cheese onto his plate, "that's what we've got!"

"Vera!"

"Yea, Joe," she said slightly distressed.

"Don't serve the fucking cheese! Its for the Outhouse," he explained as patiently as he knew she needed to hear, "pack it up and set it behind the counter."

"Oh, ok," she said picking it off the bruised boozer's plate and out of his grubby hands.

"I don't eat that crap no how," he muttered, "plugs up the pipes."

Seeing that his deodorant was also missing from atop the counter, Joe looked around and spotted one bleary-eyed sodden customer dabbing it into his coffee.

"What the hell are you doing with my *Old Spice*?" he cried taking the bottle away from him and handing him a creamer from the next table.

"I'm sorry, Joe," Vera confessed, "I wasn't watching."

"I'll be upstairs," he said closing the door to the hall and pocketing his deodorant with the sitar rhythm of a Jewish dirge on coke creeping up the stairs behind him as the Rolling Stones' morbid anthem *Paint it Black* echoed out from the bar.

He knocked on Julia's door.

"Who is it?" she asked.

"Its me, Joe. Open up."

"With flowers and my love …"

The door swung open and was shut again as soon as he had entered.

"…both never to come back," the melodic eulogy lamented its way through the floor.

"I've got the tent," he said.

"Good," Shade replied grabbing it from him, "help me wrap the fucker in it while he's still unconscious so I can carry his sorry ass out without leaving bits of him everywhere."

The mess in the bathtub bounced red light back at them in bright contrast to the shower's white surface as they wrapped the green canvas tent around their patient. When they had him packed, and Julia had checked the hall to see it was safe, Shade picked up his load in one heave and swung it onto his shoulder.

"Take the room to harpic's," he said, "then use the Thompson's from the Outhouse, just in case."

"Sure," Joe replied recognizing the need to disinfect the room of any traces of blood.

He turned to his clean up crew for the job and fetched his bucket from the corner of the room. In the two months since his recruitment by Shade, Joe's time was shared between training for the job and exercising his go'fer skills. Aside from the usual routine of replenishing the beer fridge and making runs into town, he was often left alone with his crew cleaning up whatever mess was either too disgusting or too violent for their aging maid. This not being the first grim room he was expected to cleanse of crime he grabbed the gore tinged towel from the sink and swabbed what he could with that, soaking up the puddle of antipathy and washing it down the shower's redeeming drain. Then he rinsed the bathtub as he was filling his bucket and sopped his mop in it before giving the floor a second swipe so that in less than half an hour the room was clean enough to pass a cursory inspection. Tucking his crew safely under his arm he marched out, bucket in hand, and headed downstairs being careful to lock the door behind him.

Keeping his mandate in mind, and thoughts for the sorry sinner Shade slung over his shoulder, Joe sang along with Bobby Fuller's cover of *I Fought the Law* as he headed down the stairs in the expectation that the months of waiting would culminate into something he could finally bring home.

"I left my girl and it feels so bad, I guess my race is run."

"Hi, Joe."

It was Mattie, their second waitress who usually came in later in the evening. There were only two regulars in the bar, slouched over their beer mugs and staring absently at the wall, so the girls took the opportunity to slug it out in what looked like an impromptu dance competition mixing the twist with the swim and the mashed potato.

"Hi, Mattie," he said, "seen Shade?"

"Nope," he heard her say in mid-monkey motion, "might be out back."

"Come on, Joe," Vera urged him to drop his bucket and join them as he pried himself away.

Evading her gyrations, twisting his way past, eager to know the what's, where's and why's of Julia's odd lodger, he yanked the door-knob that led to the backroom where he posted the blood and puke crew, leaving it ready for future deployment, and bounded out again this time through the rear door which led to the Outhouse. The early afternoon heat was dulled slightly by an easy breeze that played through Joe's growing hair and as he approached Shade's house, still a hundred yards away, he recognized the only person to whom his boss had ever been deferential. The one percenter tyrant's long black hair and filthy beard concealed the many scars that formed his fearsome leather mask as he kicked his heavy hog into gear and started off towards the highway with his corps close behind him. Joe waved one long hail to the entire squad as they passed by and got a nod from the last then squinted in the lifting dust that rose up after them.

Intent on finding the Thompson's before being told again, and hoping he might chance upon some clue that might explain what was going on, Joe marched into the house and headed straight for the basement where he expected Shade would be interrogating the intruder. Once inside, he found the house was quiet enough for him to continue hearing the fading final chords from the bar as the song died out just as he stepped through the basement door and started to climb down the stairs. Halfway down he surveyed the area and, finding no one near the work-bench, except for the cat whose litter he still hadn't disposed of, and certain that Shade would be grilling his guest in the back of his bunker, Joe hazarded a short distance along the dug-out trench corridor to better hear the faint voices that came from that direction.

"When's your boss gonna get here?"

"Tonight," was the pleading reply, "I told you. I've told you everything I know. I gotta pick up the girls in Vancouver..."

"When?" Shade stood over him with the empty can of gasoline threatening to set alight his incendiary infused civilian detainee.

"Tonight!" screeched the hostage, "please, don't burn me, man! please! just let me go..."

Joe knew it was unlikely that Shade would set the man on fire, at least not in his own basement, and the gasoline was just a scare tactic to make sure he got the fear fueled facts.

"Where?" Shade articulated slowly, "tell me again."

Vapor fumes set rheums streaking from his nose as he choked out another plea.

"At Vancouver International! Its all on the paper you found! I wrote my instructions down! You already know all this," his head bowed and he began to sob between gasping chokes.

Shade dropped the can of gasoline and wheeled the would-be driver into the concrete sound-proof cage, where Joe used to bunk less than a month before, and locked him in the cold damp dark to shiver away his fear. The clang of the door warned Joe of his boss' approach. Retreating to the shelved bottles of toxin, poison & bane, he feigned his search for the water sealant there and waited until Shade appeared into the work-shop's light and called him from his quest.

"Joe!" he said, "I've got something for you."

His young apprentice dropped some rags into a bucket and stepped forward.

"Yea, Frank," he said looking eager to learn more, "what is it?"

"You know what's going on?"

"No," he answered plainly, "but I did see Sonny on his way out the drive. What's up?"

"We've got a fish on the line," Shade began to explain, "This could be a big deal, something we were waiting for. Our friends got an offer from some guy in Thailand sez his shipment of heroin's comin' over by boat. Normally they wouldn't have nothing to do with no monkey off no fucking boat, but this Thai's H is V.C. so …"

"So we finally scored!"

"Not yet," Shade was glad for his enthusiasm despite being interrupted, "and its not a sure thing either but we can lock on to 'em, and see how far up this goes."

"yea," Joe became giddy with excitement.

"With a little help from Washington, the name of this Thai's driver got to us in time for me to pull him out of a wreck before the locals picked him up and ruined everything."

"So what's the gag?" Joe's enthusiasm demanded more, "Driver?! What's he driving to?"

"Three women are gonna land at Vancouver International tonight expecting to be driven to Frisco by this driver here," he said, "but they don't even know what he looks like. So we're gonna pick 'em up."

"Vancouver? Canada?" Joe asked, "who are they?"

"Get packin' kid," Shade ordered, "you're driving out to…"

A knock at the door upstairs drew their attention away. Unsure what to expect Shade reached for his shoulder holstered Browning and soft-shoed his way to the stairs.

"Frank?" Julia called, "are you here? There's a cop at the front office."

"Down here," he shouted out and heard her approaching the stairs.

She stooped below the ceiling after venturing a few steps.

"Cops are here," she said crossing her arms and sitting on the stairs, "what should I tell 'em?"

"What do they want?"

"You sponsored a soft-ball team?" she asked.

Relieved that the cop's presence had nothing to do with the day's turn eased his nerves and he nodded to her on his way up to settle the Gas Light's charitable promises.

"Alright," he said, "I'll be right there. Help Joe get ready."

"He'll be driving?" she asked.

"Yea," Shade answered, "clean'em up. Shave and a hair-cut."

Chapter 15

THE COUNTER-REVOLUTION

JOE TWISTED THE HANDLE OFF the safety-razor and fished the blade out of the sink when it fell off the end. It was old and dull, disposable, sold in little metallic boxes that kept the new ones sharp and the used ones aside until they're all too blunt for use and finally discarded. He picked up the horse-haired brush and the soap-cup off the shelf then whipped the dried and dusty shaving cake into a light lather before smearing it over his dark whiskers. Taking the next blade from his small store, he recruited a fresh new edge and screwed it to place, scraped himself a new face and threw the old mug aside smeared into a soapy towel.

The months of accumulated crud clinging to his clothes fell to the tiles by the tub along with the rags onto which it still clung. He ran the shower and retracted his hand from the cold spray then stepped beyond the plastic curtain and bore the shower's chill until it warmed. With suds foamed into his hair he rinsed off the worst of the thin mud encrusted at the roots then lathered again and attacked the filmy grime that still covered the rest of his body with the hirsute soap someone had left in the dish hanging from the moldy wall.

Clean once again he stopped the torrent and discovered a fresh towel next to the sink then dried himself off with it and tied the sopping rag around his waist as he wandered into the hall looking for Julia. She had a stool set out in the living room ready for him with comb and scissors at hand, Shade's stained table cloth slung over her shoulder and business on her mind.

"Frank's gonna be expecting you in the yard right away so I'll just give you a quick buzz-cut."

"Whatever," Joe said with no care for the style of his hair, submitting it to her leisure.

With every snip of her scissors the trappings of a false rebellion floated down and gathered on the floor to be swept away. Julia's experienced hands quickly clipped his coif and straightened his pate so that he was ready to dress again in the time it takes to recite the Star Spangled Banner in one's head.

"There you go, soldier-boy," she laughed, "you're all set."

He hopped off the stool with a pride filled grin and said, "ready for deployment," as he bounced his way to his room on the second floor of Shade's aging house and when he came back down, only minutes later, he had on a set of urban camouflage that consisted of a clean pair of straight cut gray cotton trousers, a plain white tee-shirt and an old pair of comfortable sneakers. Eager to be on his way, he stepped into the kitchen where a minor culinary commotion was underway.

"I've got your lunch," Julia said.

"You cook?" he asked not expecting her to be so viand versed as she appeared beneath her apron.

"I had three bratty brothers," she shrugged, "someone had to set them off to school."

"Joe!" Shade summoned from the door then marched into the kitchen and found the pair packing sandwiches into a cardboard box at double time, "Joe! Let's go, grab your lunch. We gotta run."

A half empty bottle of flat pop from the fridge fell into the boxed lunch along with stale chips and two apples. Joe took up the provisions and followed Shade out the door letting it slap the frame noisily on his way. The blue Volkswagon bus Shade reserved for rainy day deliveries was idling by the stairs. He threw their lunch into the back and took the passenger seat then watched Shade pull out a map from behind the wheel.

"I've outlined your route. You're gonna drive north on highway 5. Its bran' new and there might be construction along the way but buddy tells me the two lanes they've got open are pretty good all the way through Oregon, so you won't have no trouble. Then when you get to Canada, you tell them that you're going sight-seeing. Its still tourist season so they shouldn't ask too many questions. You got your I.D.?"

"Yea," Joe said slapping the wallet in his pocket.

"No drugs? No guns? Nothing?"

"No," Joe assured him.

"Good," Shade trusted him, "here's some money and the directions once you get to Vancouver International. Gate and time of arrival. All you need to get there and find 'em."

He folded the map so that the Bay area was visible then handed it to his subordinate.

"Remember they're expecting you. You're there to drive them. You look the part, now you gotta play it right too," Shade spoke quickly. "Julia's gonna be at the house and I'll call in every couple of hours so if there's a problem you leave the message with her and we'll c'ordinate from there."

Joe studied the map and read the notes over as Shade elaborated his instructions.

"You got it?"

His accomplice had to blink to assure himself he understood the instructions.

"What do I do when I've picked them up?" he asked finding a void in his preparation.

Shade took up the notes and turned to the second page, "here's the address of the motel outside Vancouver where you're gonna take them. The owner's a friend of ours, you take them there and tell them your name at the office and they'll give you two rooms. These women won't be looking to run away or make trouble if they trust you so you just set 'em up in their room and don't worry about nothin'. In the morning you'll pack them in the truck again and drive down to San Francisco but this time you go down this old road across the border where our guy'll be stationed that knows us. He'll just wave you through."

Joe flipped to the third page of his notes, read the directions there then found the small border crossing outlined on the map and nodded his comprehension.

"You got it?"

"Yea."

"Alright," Shade opened the door and let Joe take his place, "you're not late but you can't be too long on the road."

The engine shook the van into motion and as the dust kicked up behind him Joe turned onto the highway heading north towards San Francisco and the Bay Bridge to Oakland. With the wind rustling through his opened window he turned on the radio and the Beatles *Paperback Writer* came to life. When the song ended the animated DJ, whose station was promoting the Beatles tour-ending show at Candlestick Park later that evening, sent out urgent pleas inciting everyone to come out despite the recent masses of anti-Beatles protests that continued to burn across the country. The show's expected attendance was uncertain.

As he sped north along the bay towards the city Joe could see the San Francisco International Airport up ahead, extraction point for the vanguard force of the British Invasion, and flower armed hippies communing along the side of the road on their way to the home of giants would witness the end of an era.

A comment buried in the text of a long rambling interview which was ignored in the UK, "we're bigger than Jesus," incited a conflagration of biblical proportions in America when newspapers headlined those same words in capital black print across their front pages months after they had been spoken.

And the counter-revolution had begun.

In the land of the free, daily threats reached the English gurus of love and long hair as they found themselves attacked by the mobs which only an orchestrated barrage of propaganda could summon, and the masters of religious intolerance intimidated a once unretractable artist into apologizing. The impending break-up of rock'n-roll's great mop-heads loomed.

Small bands of guitar wielding revolutionaries intent on changing the world with song marched across the Bay Bridge on a pilgrimage sipping ablutions to their heroes unaware of the darker forces that were already mobilized against them. Joe rounded the interchange in Oakland and passed over the University Avenue exit recalling stories of the first sign the revolution would be attacked. Winston Churchill's V-for-Victory, subverted by America's love-revolution, was prominently displayed at anti-war protests forcing the powers of the long existing hierarchy to defend themselves against the threat which an independent youth movement represented. In a yet unpublished letter to the president of the United States, a hardened biker element was offered as a fighting unit to combat behind enemy lines in Vietnam. Though the official reply from the American president's office suggested these men don their country's uniform and enroll into the armed forces like any other recruit, only months after the missive had received its postal seal, a leather-clad crew in full-patch gear wielding chains and clubs stormed from behind a police barricade and attacked a group of protesters at Berkeley, still adhering to the belief that a violent assault would staunch the demonstrations. But violence does not silence an ideological insurgency. This is a fact which the rebel signatories to America's secession from England recognized when they watched the revolutionary capital of Philadelphia fall to the hands of the British, a fact which dawned on the nation's powers again when the brutal counter-revolutionary reprisal meted out against the Berkeley protesters of 1966 incited the Beat poet Allen Ginsberg to moderate the mutiny with the appeasing slogan *Flower Power*.

And a new tactic needed be employed.

If drugs could be used to control the minds of patients in clinical tests the mass dissemination of hallucinogens, downers & opiates could be expected to have a deterring effect on the youth leaders and their legions of followers. And so the ostentatious displays of habitual usage by the heroes of the disenfranchised made them billboards of marketing for the chemical weapons intended to neutralize the dynamics of disaffection while providing plausible means of destroying those who persistently preached against the moral authority of the state. To promote this stratagem and encourage the would be philosophers away from their classrooms and into the dulling halls of narcotics, a respected Harvard professor of psychology, Dr.Timothy Leary, will step forward with the attractive summon to "Tune in, Turn on and Drop out".

But Pfeizer, Bayer and Merke-Frost could not peddle to the poor in Haight-Ashbury or Greenwich Village like an armed biker corporation could so the motorcycle underworld will be commissioned to profit from the subjugation of the pacifist insurrection. And because raising one demon to roam unchecked is an even greater danger than the threat of a free-willed population, a Texas club will rise to rival California's. Where there are two, there will soon be a third and the biker-wars over America's drug-trade will eventually attain a tolerable coexistence in a stable balance of power somewhere beneath the authority that encouraged their growth and above the plebeians who bled for their profit.

It will take years for the effects of this strategy to be felt. Before this will happen the Beatles manager Brian Epstein will die of a drug overdose. Three days at Woodstock will prove that the peaceniks can assemble en masse if left to themselves, inciting a racial slur to riot the guardians of Altamont out of control and bring an end to the party. As the evening of the sixties will wane, night will fall over America with the Tate murders and a mythologized *hippie guru* by the name of Charles Manson will appear in the popular conscience. Fall further into night with the deaths of Jones, Hendrix and Joplin, who will either drown themselves while on drugs or drown themselves with drugs, all at the height of their popularity. And by morning, Jim Morrison, the once telegenic but now bearded fattened and drunken pop poet and lizard king will fail in his Paris apartment too bored with the mindless idolatry that will take over what should have always been a movement of ideals.

Joe veered the Volkswagon towards the brown shirted Canadian border-guard that invited him to his gate.

"Good evening, sir. May I see your driver's license and registration? And where will you be traveling? How long do you plan on staying? Do you have anything to declare before entering into Canada? Thank you, and enjoy your stay."

Chapter 16

ISLAND AIRPORT

IN THE DARKENING EVENING JOE could barely make out the wooded scenery that sped by along the highway to Vancouver. The city lay ahead and for some time there was little traffic besides his van making the journey north with him and soon the rural setting restyled itself into a series of sprawling suburban neighborhoods that stretched away from urbanity. As he approached the city's limits he checked his speed and assumed a place in traffic while navigating towards the island airport south of town getting to the parking lot wicket, where he received his voucher from a tired attendant, only half an hour before the three women he was sent to pick up were scheduled to arrive from Bangkok. Turning into the near empty lot, he parked a short distance away from the international gates entrance then rifled through his notes to find the hand-printed sign with the family's name on it which their original driver had intended to use to identify himself with. The sign in hand, Joe made a quick inspection of the van to be certain it was not littered with any trash that might offend his passengers by packing what he did find into his cardboard lunch-box, then he closed and locked the doors and marched towards the airport leaving the trash by a convenient bin at the terminal doors.

When he stepped into the building he at first listened to the arrivals and departures being announced and, failing to understand the garbled voice coming through the intercom, determined his best course of action would be to find the gate where they were destined to appear and inquire about the flight's schedule there. He made his way the short distance to the designated waiting area without difficulty and found only late stragglers from an earlier flight still lingering around the luggage carousel. The chalkboard behind the counter announcing the Bangkok flight's scheduled arrival time had not been altered and he found himself a place near the gate. Knowing only that there were three women arriving from Thailand, he was uncertain what to look for and merely stood near the exit waiting with their name clearly printed and legible in his hands for everyone to read.

Others soon arrived and waited alongside of him to greet their guests and relatives who were also traveling from Thailand as the tired and dreary passengers began to trickle out of the gate and were promptly greeted by long-missed loved ones relieved to see them arrive safely. Only now remembering that he would likely need a cart for their baggage Joe thrust his hand into his pocket to measure the amount of change he held there and assumed that the jingling tinkling sound he heard sufficed, easing his worries. He then turned his attention to the gate once more looking for three disoriented women who might recognize the name printed on the cardboard he held in his hand. Among the laggard faces that eagerly scoured the crowd for a friendly reception he found a tired looking middle aged woman of sleight stature in a light summer dress who looked awkwardly out of place clinging to her relatively bulky suitcase. She caught sight of Joe's gaze as they made eye-contact then perused the sign in his hand without recognizing the name written on it. Disappointed that he had not yet located his passengers, Joe looked further beyond the gate hoping he might there find his three women from Thailand.

Scanning the back of a floral patterned dress, Joe's attention was firmly riveted on the slender shape around which its bright colored efflorescence formed itself. Following the curves of her back up to her neck the golden Venus of the Orient turned towards him sensing the permissiveness with which he allowed himself to stare. Finally withdrawing his attention from the reverie that so sudden an exposure to the raptures which he imagined the garden of delights had to offer, Joe smiled innocently hoping she was a member of his party but was disappointed when she too looked at his sign and turned her head away.

After being so repugnantly dismissed, Joe surveyed the wayfaring factions that began to field the baggage carousel and heard a peeling squeal from beneath the crowd speaking a quick and erratic foreign tongue while distinctly repeating the name written on the board in his hands. As the crowds passed by the diminutive voice soon piped up at him from between strolling travelers where he found its source in pristine white dress, patent leather shoes and pig tails.

"Hi," she said in perfect english, "we're the Noni's."

She turned to look behind her expecting her family to be there and was surprised to see no one she recognized then ran off again. Taking his cue to follow after the black-haired fairy, Joe parted through the mob under which she slipped away and paused in mid-search to hear her voice again then caught a similar babel issuing from the comely flower who'd dismissed him the moment before. When he reached the chittering threesome, whom he expected, the determined mien on the face of their elder was only slightly colder than the glare he met in the tired brown eyes of his Asian dream. Only the younger of the three peered up at him with a welcoming smile.

"Hello," he said as he extended his hand to their mother, "my name is Joe. Mr.Noni hired me to take you to a hotel for the night and drive you safely to San Francisco in the morning."

"No inglis," she said with a shake of her head turning to the child between them.

"My mother doesn't speak any english, mister," she explained, "neither does my sister, Mekhla. But mother asked me to tell you that we are ready to go to the hotel."

Joe smiled politely and tucking the cardboard that had served its purpose beneath his arm he reached for Mrs.Noni's suitcase and was repudiated when the woman held on to it shaking her head, a gesture he took to understand that she would carry it herself. Retracting his hand and making as passive a gesture of obeisance as western culture allowed he made the same offer to the older daughter who reluctantly deigned to forfeit the charge of the heavy handbag strung onto her shoulder. Happy to oblige, Joe took the load from the lovely asiatic lass and straightened his back hoping to promote the image of honest courtesy which he wished to impart then got his instructions from their young interpreter to escort them to their chariot.

"My mother says you should take us to the hotel now," she repeated.

He looked on the ground around them wondering if they had anymore bags for him to carry and finding none he asked, "should we not find the rest of your luggage?"

"That's all we brought," the inky haired lily replied, "father will bring the rest of our things with him."

"Ok," he said leaning towards the exit and inviting them to follow while listening to their whispered lyrical dialect trying to imagine what they were saying in tones that varied from grievous to sing-song until the little one probed him with the results of their parley.

"We're all a bit hungry," she said in a slightly plaintive manner that was also endearing, "my mother would like to know where we could find something to eat."

"There will be food at the hotel," he said with a congenial smile directed at their mother, "but we can stop by a drive-thru along the way if you like."

"Drive-thru! I've heard of those," cheered his translator, "all my friends at school tell me they're really good. Can we go to one of those?"

Joe was pleasantly taken aback by the excitement that bubbled out of his young ward who was apparently the only one of the three who had slept on the plane.

"Sure. We're bound to find something you like," he said then had to reflect on what he knew of the eating habits of Thai's, "you're not vegetarians are you?"

"My sister is," she said.

"Mekhla?" Joe asked to be certain he remembered the girl's name properly.

"Yea," came the merry reply as she skipped along beside him, "my name's Intira but you can call me *Inti* 'cos that's what my friends call me."

He smiled at her exuberance then worried for the lassitude that seemed to overtake her parent and sibling.

"Its a pleasure to meet you, Inti. My name is Joseph but

you can call me *Joe* 'cos that's what my friends call me," he said surprised to be taking her hand when they reached the exit and the darkness outness incited it to involuntarily find his.

He pushed his way through twisting himself around while holding the door for the others to follow and then, with a reassuring wink, led them to the nearby van. Chilled by the night air the tired travelers shivered as they kept pace with him while he tried to comfort the handsome threesome with pleasant sounding platitudes of the warmth and ease that awaited them at the hotel while surveying the few people laboring to and from the airport.

"This is it," he said when they reached the blue van and he was fishing his keys from his pocket and opening the side door.

"Can I sit in the front?" asked Inti.

"Sure," Joe replied as the little white frill flushed past her sister and dove into the van clamoring for the front passenger seat, "if its alright with your mother."

Once Inti was comfortably mounted there and no one showed any concern for the seat she had chosen for herself Joe felt a hand on his shoulder and turned to help Mrs.Noni struggle aboard while she still clung to her cumbersome suitcase. When she too was settled aboard, apparently now more serene in her seat than she had been up until that moment, the only remaining concern was in the amount of assistance the uprooted raven-haired flourish standing beside him needed. He offered her his hand and she found a seat in the dignified way which her lithe appearance required allowing Joe to wrest her hand-bag off his shoulder and set it onto the floor of the van beside her.

He gently closed the door, not wishing to startle his

passengers, and rounded the vehicle while keeping an eye out for anyone suspicious in the area. Aside from an elderly couple, who looked like they were reunited with their balding middle-aged son, there appeared to be little for him to be concerned about. He opened the driver side door, climbed aboard, and found Inti sitting poised beside him with her hands resting on her knees grinning at the rain splotches in the windscreen and the gray night beyond. Wrapping himself around his seat to inspect the pair sitting behind him he discovered Mekhla resting her head on her mother's shoulder while the matriarch kept a stern watch over her two daughters.

He smiled pleasantly at the grave matron then turned the key in the ignition and started them on their way. As cautious in his driving as his living cargo was precious, Joe rendered the parking fare at the exit while listening to the little locutionist in the adjacent seat.

"What's that loud noise?" she asked referring to the jet planes overhead, "sounds like a giant cat purring in my ear."

"That's just a plane like the one you were on earlier," he replied while negotiating the next turn, "do you like cats?"

"We've never had a cat at home, mother doesn't like them very much, but Tabby shared our dorm with us at my school in Zurich. The sisters said he was a good *mouser*."

"The sisters!? You're Catholic?"

"Yep," she answered without concern, "we used to be Buddhist but I don't really know what that means. Only that since we're Catholic I get to go to school in Zurich. Have you ever been to Zurich?"

"No," he said, "it must be nice over there."

Chapter 17

PANCAKE BREAKFAST

When morning came Joe's reveille rang through the telephone. Having enjoyed the luxury of a late-night James Cagney movie on the black-and-white television that came with the elevated price of a single occupancy, his groggy mind took a moment to focus while his head rested on the down pillow until dream merged with life and he sprang to his post holding the receiver to his ear.

"Hello?" he said with alarm.

"Hey, Joe," Shade spoke through the line, "everythin' ok?"

"Uh," he had to wipe the webs of rest aside before reflection could progress beyond monosyllabic non-discourse, "yea. Yea."

"Are you alright?"

"Yea," he said regaining the power of speech along with reason and self-assurance, "I just got up. Things went well last night. I picked them up, we grabbed something to eat at a drive-thru and then I drove them to the hotel. The hotel's manager was expecting us, like you said, and handed me the keys to these two adjacent rooms. They're still in there sleeping right now. I'm right next to them and I didn't hear a thing all night. Everything's great."

The line went quiet for a few moments.

"Frank? Are you there?"

"Yea, Joe," Shade finally broke the silence, "you should look in on 'em. They might be jet-lagged."

"I'll shower and go see, I don't want to wake them."

"Don't take too long. You gotta be at the border between nine 'n ten this morning. You know how long it takes you to get there?"

"Sure," Joe reassured him, "we'll have a late breakfast and then head out."

"They won't give you any trouble?"

"No," he replied pleased with himself, "everything's fine."

"Ok, that's good. Some friends'll ride back with ya, you just follow the road and everythin'll work out fine but don't take too long to get going. And have a look in on 'em soon."

"Right away," Joe said standing to attention until he was dismissed and hung up the phone.

The morning television programming had come on to replace the static that had fused with the morpheus muse and a local cooking program vaunted the benefits of salmon in a family's weekly diet when he turned off the tv and removed his socks on his way to the shower. The morning cleansing ritual that life at the Gas Light effaced was gladly taken up again. He stripped down and enjoyed a zesting start to his day under the warm wet spray then quickly rinsed and toweled himself dry. Making some effort to wipe the wrinkles out of his pants he considered letting them drink in the damp dew of a steaming shower but his pending redeployment pressed him to dress and so he hastened to break camp.

Dressed in his new urban fatigues again he looked in the mirror to be certain he maintained the same trustworthy appearance he had the night before and then knocked onto the door to the adjacent room. Hearing no commotion from within he waited for them to rise then knocked again when no one came in answer to his first summons but still got no response the second time. As his concern to see the mission completed grew to alarm he darted through the front door of his room into the carpeted hallway and found that the *Do Not Disturb* sign he had left on the handle to the Noni family's hotel room door was missing. He struggled to maintain a reasonable level of calm but found himself furiously banging on their door anxious to get a response. When none came he raced down to the office to speak with the manager, the only member of the hotel personnel aware of the family's importance.

He was certain that they could not have wandered very far on their own. Hoping to find them comfortably seated at a table in the restaurant, though the maple syrup breakfast advertised by the eatery's door was not the usual morning fare in Thailand, he peered into the modest dining room anyway and caught the smell of canadian bacon without a hint of his three missing charges then dashed to the front desk to inquire there. When the manager was not at the desk Joe found that the morning's business was in the hands of a subordinate whose pleasant greeting failed to palliate his concerns.

"Good morning, sir," she said having seen him enter the lobby from the stairs, "are you leaving us already?"

"I need to speak to the manager," he said with his nervous sweaty hand pressed against the top of the counter.

"I'm sorry, sir, but the manager is unavailable at the moment. Perhaps I may be of some assistance," she replied sensing the urgency of his request.

"When will he be back?" he asked, "do you have any way to reach him?"

"The floor manager has stepped out on a pressing matter for another guest but you can leave a message if you like. I'll be sure to have him call your room when he arrives."

"Ok, but can you tell me if you've seen two women and a young girl leave the hotel this morning?"

"I started my shift less than an hour ago and to my knowledge, sir, all the guests who have come down from the suites are now sitting in the restaurant."

"You're sure?"

"I've only been here about forty minutes," she said turning his attention to the clock on the wall, "the morning shift started at eight o'clock and the staff that was here overnight has already left."

"So you don't know?" he pointed out to her with some level of drama.

"Do you know what room they're in? They may have checked out already."

"Room 214," he said, "the one adjoining mine. We're on the same bill."

She looked at the room keys hanging on the wall behind her and said, "they haven't returned their key but if you give me a moment I will have a look at our records." Noticing nothing in the lengthy ledger before her she verified the room's mail slot and found it bare then perused a filing cabinet for the family's card and apologized once more, "I'm sorry, sir. We have no record of their leaving. Perhaps they've gone out for a walk. Have you tried the park?"

"No," he said taking samples of the hospitality pamphlets on her desk thinking they could lead him to them, "what park?"

"There's a soft-padded path around the grounds that leads through our beautiful garden and a small play-park for children near the pool. All of our guests are welcomed to use the facilities. Its such a beautiful day outside, its quite possible they may simply have gone for a walk."

"Thank you," he said.

Bounding out the front door of the lobby he found himself standing at the top of a short flight of stairs that led to the building's parking lot and scanned the distance to either side hoping to find them sitting quietly together on a bench but instead only managed to surprise a pair of brown squirrels scurrying about the greenery. On the edge of the lot, beside the taxi stand, he noticed a white painted sign with directions to the pool inviting him along a forested path. The thick foliage that prevented him from seeing beyond the first curve of the deliberately winding way designed to create intimacy at every turn forced him to quicken his pace and race through what would otherwise have been a pleasant walk. The relatively short path seemed infinitely long to him as he ran past the empty benches along the hotel's flower garden and botanical embrasure towards a gated children's play-park.

There he thought of asking a young mother, who sat by the jungle gym watching over her toddler while reading a brightly colored magazine, whether she had seen the women he was looking for but decided against it and looked over the pool instead. It was still too early for most bathers and no life-guard was yet on duty so he rounded his search of the park with a brief look at the far side of the shuttered canteen's half dozen tables and raced back the way he came foiled in his search and anxious to start again on a different lead.

Pulling the pamphlets out of his back pocket he felt certain that they had not gone to the Hastings Racecourse and threw that one aside. The idea that they may have taken a boat tour was somewhat less frightening than a possible abduction but he was reluctant to admit either scenario and ran out towards the parking lot again where a taxi was arriving to drop guests off at the front door. With the hopes that they could be returned to his charge safely and in the comforts of a Co-oP cab defying his fears, he spotted two dark heads sitting inside it when it rolled by. He stared intently at their backs, worrying that he may be wrong but certain that he wasn't, eager to know if these dark haired creatures were indeed two of the threesome which had so unnerved him, a third jet-head with a bright cheery face popped up from between the others and waved to him through the rear window beneath her bouncing pig-tails.

The passenger side door opened and Mekhla's slender calf stretched itself out as he appeared next to the cab with an extreme sense of relief taking hold of him. He peered through the front window and offered the driver five dollars for their fare then refused to take his change and found the three delinquent daughters of Thailand smiling and refreshed beside him.

"Hi, Joe," said Inti without a moment's pause, "where were you this morning? We knocked on your door and you didn't answer."

"Is that right? I must have been in the shower," he explained before asking, "where did you all go to?"

"Mother wanted to take us to church," she answered

enjoying the pleasure of taking his hand and leading him inside.

"But how did you find a church?" he asked.

"We asked the taxi driver to find us one and then I told him mother wanted him to pick us up after the service," she said bouncing beside him, "we're going to have pancakes now!"

"Do they have pancakes in Thailand?" he asked thrilled to see them all in such a good mood.

"I don't know," she shrugged, "but the sisters served us some one time and they were great!"

Inti ran off ahead of them to read the breakfast menu advertised outside the restaurant door as he waved to the desk clerk who was putting down her phone, and they were soon seated by the same waitress that took their order. After listening to the pleasant sounding conversation which Mekhla and her mother shared while eating their grapefruits, and when they had all finished their coffees, the bill was his for him to take and they headed upstairs to their rooms where he found their only suitcase already packed.

"If your mother and sister are ready," he said to his interpreter, "tell them we need to be on our way."

Translating the instructions she got from her mother Inti asked, "You're going to drive us to San Francisco now?"

"Yes," he replied in as congenial a tone as possible, "We mustn't leave too late, its a long drive."

The brief explanation that followed incited her sister to offer him her bag to carry and they all followed after him towards the lobby where he returned the room keys at the front desk.

"I hope you've enjoyed your stay," said the exuberant clerk from behind the counter.

"Thank you," Joe replied still feeling elated and relieved from his earlier worries, "we certainly did."

"Loved your pancakes," shouted the little gourmande pushing through the exit.

Chapter 18

SECRET ASIAN MAN

JOE SHUT MEKHLA AND HER mother into the back of the van, looked in on Inti sitting in the front then made a quick inspection of the vehicle before climbing in the driver's seat.

"I have to make a quick phone call," he said to his co-pilot as she scoured over the map, "you got our route all figured out?"

"I'm working on it," she said after a brief deliberation, "looks like we go through Blaine."

"Yea, it does doesn't it?" the engine turned and in a minute they were on the road looking for a gas station, "we'll make a short stop at a gas station and then we head to San Francisco."

"Ok," his navigator approved so entranced by the details of their trip she didn't look up from the map until they were stopped at a pumping station. "Wow! Are those motorcycles?"

"Yep," Joe said recognizing some of Sonny's crew waiting to escort them home, "looks like they're gonna ride along with us. Won't that be nice?"

"So long as they don't make any trouble," she said with a hint of disapproval.

"I'm sure they won't," Joe replied as the gas station attendant came to his window, "fill'er-up and check the oil."

"Yes, sir."

The three disheveled rough-hands sat astride their iron rides idling in a dull purr without acknowledging the presence of the van and Joe stepped out when the opened hood obstructed their view inside.

"I'm just going to use the phone for a second," he repeated to Inti a third time then nodded pleasantly to the pair in the back seat and crossed the station's lot to the phone. "Operator? Yes, a grocery store in Blaine please."

He dropped the requisite coins in the slot and waited.

"Hello, I'm driving through town and need provisions. Do you sell sandwiches? and salads? Great. Anything vegetarian? Ok, four of those. Some egg, tuna. Give me a mix. Yes. About twelve, no, make that fifteen sandwiches. A dozen colas, water. Mixed. A dozen. Some nuts. Sure. Yea. I'll pick it up. Where are you? Hazelmere & 203rd. Excellent. No, I'm in Vancouver, on the road. Just the time it takes me to drive. I will. Hazelmere & 203rd, yes ma'am. and thank you."

He hung up and paid for the gas then approached the captain of the cruel cavalry.

"We gotta stop for provisions on Hazelmere and 203rd," he said, "you know how to get there?"

"Yea, its on the way to the border," came the self-assured reply, "forty minutes. Less if there's no traffic."

"Ok but I don't want to drive too fast and upset the women," Joe insisted.

"Don't worry, we'll be doing 65 most of the way. We should be there around midnight tonight."

"Alright," he said and headed back to the van displaying a beaming smile for his passengers.

"Mother wants to know who those men are," Inti said sitting sideways.

"No need to worry," he said confidently, "these are the men your father hired to make sure you're safe. They're friends."

"Fwens?" asked Mrs.Noni in her broken english.

"Yes," he said seeing the concern lift from all their faces. "And we're off."

The iron cavalry led the way south and veered east away from the main border at the Peace Arch Provincial Park until they got to the grocery store on 203rd. After leaving the women to the care of their convoy for the time it took him to pay for the trip's provisions and return to the van, Joe stowed the bags then resumed his place behind the wheel.

"Looks like we won't need a map after all," he said pleased to see Inti grinning again.

"They sound like big roaring tigers," she said.

"They do don't they!"

"Did you buy us some pop?" she asked pivoted in her chair, "I haven't had pop since my fake birthday."

"Fake birthday?" Joe asked.

"Yes," she cheered when she spotted the caps of the pop bottles in the bag, "I love pop! Did you get the fizzy purple and the fizzy orange. Because those are the best ones."

They turned south and Joe looked at the time as they approached the gravel-road border crossing. It was barren and its barrier seemed locked upright. Then a lone-uniformed border-guard popped out of his small office and waved them through pulling the barrier down again only when they had passed.

"Joe?"

"Yea?" he asked still looking at the border guard in the rear-view mirror distractedly.

"Did you get the fizzy orange?"

"Huh? Oh, yea. I think so. I asked for a mix of flavors and most stores… Yea, I'm sure we have the fizzy orange," he said glad to have passed another hurdle. "So what's this about a fake birthday?"

"I have two birthdays," she was pleased to announce. "When we lived in Bangkok my father brought us to a party in a restaurant. A big white marbled place with fountains and everything! And some of father's friends were there with their families to celebrate victory day with us but when a table of G.I.'s came over to ask what we were all celebrating he told them that it was my birthday! He even bought me a big cake with my name on it. *Happy Birthday Inti* it said. In English! It was really funny."

"When was this?" Joe asked curious.

"A few years ago," she said, "during a spring vacation from school."

"Victory day? In Thailand? What victory were you celebrating?"

"Dienbienphu, of course," she said naively, "I had two pieces and it was really…"

Mrs.Noni's stern voice interrupted her from the back and his co-pilot began to pout then sat silent for some time. He found a Seattle radio station and watched the road as he thought about Inti and her family.

"What's a *Secret Asian Man*?" she asked in reference to the song that played.

"Secret *Agent* Man," he corrected, "have you heard of James Bond?"

"Yes," she said her excitement returning, "some of my friends talk about his movies at school. He's a spy! There are advertisements for the film *Thunderball* in all the magazines. Reviews. I've read some. He's very handsome. Is that what this song is about?"

"Yes, I guess so."

"I'd love to see his movies," she stared out dreamy eyed across the windscreen then said, "looks like its going to rain. Your friends will get wet on their motorcycles."

"They're used to it," he assured her, "besides. Its warm out."

"Not that warm," she said pretending to shiver and making him laugh.

"They'll be ok."

After a series of rounds of 20-Questions, I See and Name That License Plate sandwiches were pulled out along with orange fizzy pop. Inti eventually found a new amusing toy in the form of the radio dial as they drifted down the highway and faded in and out of each station's reception. There were long stretches of silence that was intermittently interrupted by the sparse and delicate conversation which Mekhla shared with her mother and his interpretor didn't think important enough to translate.

The girls stretched their legs and used the facilities during a brief pause at a fueling station near Albany south of Portland but their jet-lag took a fresh hold of them again before the caravan reached California, midway through their second sandwiches sometime around 2100h. Joe drowned the last swig of the flat purple drink that still remained in the bottom of the warm bottle and soon saw Oakland's glow beckon in the distant night. The effulgent sky over the city neared and soon its lights flickered past him as he fled the heavily trafficked interchange and bounded over the Bay Bridge towards San Francisco.

It was after midnight when they arrived at the Gas Light. Shade had made an effort to shave and comb back his hair but still looked of the menace genus despite his clean clothes. The hog convoy made a u-turn in the hotel's driveway as they headed back to the city and their own clubhouse leaving Joe free to shelter the girls in the relative quiet of a wednesday night road-house parking lot listening to an undistinguished ballad beyond the overheating van's tired and plaintive hum.

Mrs.Noni woke Mekhla who was sleeping leaned against her shoulder and the two women drowsily looked around uncertainly.

"We're here," Joe said to them reassuringly with Shade standing next to his door.

"Everything go alright?" Shade inquired confidentially.

"Yea," Joe assured him stepping out of the van, "are we putting them in the hotel?"

"No," he said, "Julia's got the guest room ready for 'em. Take 'em there."

Joe nodded his compliance and maintained a benevolent appearance despite the toll which the long drive had taken on his morale. Rounding the van he opened the side door and invited Mekhla to step down while Shade headed towards the bar where a new hotel patron had arrived and was heading to the front office watching them from across the parking lot.

Mekhla stood up as straight as her confines conceded then placed a foot on the running board while taking Joe's hand and felt his shoulder made a better support than the door's handle. Allowing a smile of gratitude escape from her stoic features she turned to help her mother and the two of them each took a hand to ease her onto the graveled lot.

"Hi, Joe," Julia approached from the hotel's rear entrance wearing a sober but colorful dress and smiling brightly, "are these our guests?"

"Hi, Julia, these are the Noni's. Can you help them to their room?" he asked reaching into the passenger seat to take Inti up in his arms as she slept. "They have a suitcase in the back and another bag. I'll take the little one if you can carry the suitcase."

"Sure," she said making a wide motion around Mrs.Noni to reach for the suitcase heaving it with a brimming smile.

He closed the passenger door with the napping nipper pressed against his chest and slung Mekhla's bag over his shoulder inviting her and her mother to follow him towards the house. Too tired to make any close observation of the building's exterior they let themselves be led inside and up the stairs to the guest room above. Joe gently lay Mrs.Noni's youngest daughter onto the clean covers of their bed for her to care for then made sure that Mekhla saw him open the door to the adjoining washroom and turn on the light. As he did so the tabby which Shade kept jumped out from beneath his feet with a kitten gripped by the scruff of the neck benignly dangling submissively in its mouth. Since neither Mekhla nor her mother seemed offended by the scene, Joe smiled at nature's feral maternity and watched it saunter away.

Their suitcase sat by the foot of the bed and, after closing the curtains, Julia laid three folded bathrobes out on the dresser then retreated to the door.

"I'll bring food up in a few minutes," she offered knowing not to make hand gestures to foreigners who may misinterpret her meaning. "Food," she repeated and was certain that she was vaguely understood.

"This one is vegetarian," Joe blithely announced and stepped towards the door.

"Yep, ok," Julia confirmed.

With a near kow-towing tone of deference they backed out of the room and closed the door then stood in the hallway and headed downstairs.

"How was the trip?" she asked.

"Long," he said putting his arm around her.

"I bet," she agreed, "Frank said he wants to see you in his office."

"Yea, I figured," he replied ready for a debriefing, "I'll see you later?"

"Just as soon as I get their lunch," she promised and kissed him on the neck sending him off to see Shade.

Two of the civilian clad sentries posted to the house sat relaxing at their stations near the stairs and Joe knew there would be a third garrisoned on the roof keeping a vigilant eye waiting for the shift rotation and his relief. The van was left for him to clear of junk and return to the barn, a task he'd have to do after receiving instructions from Shade. For now, he cut the idling engine, shut the doors and headed towards the Gas Light singing to himself.

"Chances are you won't live to see tomorrow."

Chapter 19

AMERICAN GOOKS

"Do they like coffee?" Julia asked.

"Black!" Joe said biting his toast & jam.

"So you don't think I made it too strong?"

"Don't worry. They had a cup for breakfast yesterday and haven't had any since. If they're in the habit of devouring eight cups a day they'll drink tar out of the ashtrays. They had one cup yesterday and not a word of it all along the ride here," Joe said allowing his own morning cup to elaborate for him.

"But do they like coffee?"

Joe shook his head and walked into the living room pretending to be annoyed by her obsession.

"Ok, I'll just take it up with their toast but if they don't like it its your fault," she said peskily as she took up the tray.

"Of course," he laughed and turned on the tv, "you can have me court-marshalled if they don't like your coffee."

A morning news program was telecasting the latest video footage depicting the muddy blood fields of Vietnam. As he sat considering what foreign deployment would have been like he munched on his toast contented by the certainty that he would eventually make his parents understand why he had made the decisions he had. But in trying to convince himself of the dignity of the part he played he only managed to remind himself of the pain he caused them. The carnage on the screen ceased long enough for a commercial break and an advertisement for school supplies at a local drug-store took him back to Pleasant Hill. He imagined Jennifer on her way to Grove's Hill without him. He could have studied engineering at M.I.T. or settled with his girl after Grove's Hill, opted for R.O.T.C. training or made a stint with a minor-league baseball team but chose instead to sully his name on a dirty posting that promised nothing but ignominy for the years that he was underground without any real certainty of public redemption.

"Shoo, shoo," Julia was coming down the stairs empty tray in hand, "there's something wrong with the cat."

"Yea," Joe said brushing his personal woes aside, "we gotta get it spayed. Its that damned litter."

"Why haven't you gotten rid of it yet? You were supposed to do that weeks ago."

He dismissed the chore every time he was reminded of it, "I'll get around to it."

"You just don't want to," she said, "do you?"

She was right.

"I'll get around to it," he repeated his empty promise, "I've just been busy."

"Uh huh," she mumbled on her way to the kitchen.

"How'd they like your coffee," he asked following after her.

"I didn't stay to watch but they seemed pleased to see me bring it in."

"Maybe the guys downstairs would like some," he suggested referring to the three civvy grunts playing cards on Shade's work-bench in the basement.

"I think they have their own," she said, "Frank doesn't want me bothering them too much."

"He's probably right about that," Joe agreed, "you know where they're going next week. They'll be looking for some American tail before they get there."

"Where is he anyway?" she asked.

"I don't know," he poured himself another cup of black java, "probably getting his ass kicked at pinnacle."

"Joe!" Shade startled him from the door.

"Yea?" he put down his cup and hopped to the common room, "what is it?"

"Sit down," Shade hurried to the coffee table and pushed an empty mug aside while Joe took a seat beside him. "I've got the details of today's delivery."

"So we're still on this? They're not taking over?"

"Not yet," he said, "we've got a friend from Washington's gonna represent Sonny at the pier and once you deliver Noni's family our business is done."

"Deliver them? To Noni? I have to deliver those women? and that little girl to this Noni character?" he asked with some disgust.

"Joe," Shade tried a light handed tactic with him, "they're his family. He's not going to fucking eat them. Just let it go and do your job. This is out of our hands."

"What's going to happen to them?" he asked.

Shade made light of his question, "what do you think is going to happen? They'll get deported and wind up stooped over a sodden rice paddy. No one's after your slit-eyed sweetie,

Joe. And you don't need to worry none about the little one neither. You just drive them to Noni, take the two keys of heroin he owes us and fuck off. Buddy from town's gonna handle the matter."

"Deported? You think they'll just be deported? We catch a Vietcong heroin dealer in San Francisco and you think he and his family are just going get deported?" he said allowing his third cup of coffee to get the better of him.

"Its over our heads, Joe," Shade put down his notes and gave him a black-eyed glared which had the desired effect of putting Joe's heels to the carpet. "Don't muddle this," he said with his clenched fists gripped tightly on the table and when the seething hiss of his voice had finished spitting out the last syllable through clenched teeth, he added, "and keep your voice down."

Bowed by rank and cowed by force, Joe refrained from falling out further and retracted himself, "Yes, sir."

"Ok, then," Shade continued his briefing and pushed the map in front of Joe, "here's the pier off The Embarcadero, you've been through there a couple of times on jobs before. You drive through the gate and straight to the pier where he'll be waiting for you," he pointed to the map. "Got it?"

Joe pulled the chart closer.

"Drive up to the pier and deliver the girls. Don't try to negotiate, just park and let them out when they see their V.C. pappy."

"I got it," he said angrily, "then what?"

"Then, when they're reunited with Daddy-deals-drugs, you take the two keys of heroin and say, 'this man speaks for Sonny' in way of introducing our buddy-from-town."

"And then?"

145

"And then you leave," Shade finished.

"That's it?"

"That's it. You deliver the girls and introduce our guy to Dok Noni, then you take the heroin and the job is done."

Joe's head stalled for thought then bowed into subjection, "ok."

"The Company's arrived. He's waiting outside right now ready to go."

"When's this gonna happen?"

"Pack them up, you've got half an hour to get going," Shade commanded. "Get Julia to help you. I'm sure they're anxious to get out of here. So half an hour should be plenty of time to get them in the van."

"Ok," Joe waited for further instructions.

"Go! Now, get on with it!"

He jumped to his feet and spotted Julia closing the basement door and shooing the cat down.

"Julia!" he said, "we have to get the girls ready. Can you come upstairs."

"Coming," she managed the door and dashed through the kitchen to catch up with him, "is it time yet?"

"Yea, help me get them in the van," he said climbing the stairs on his way to the guest room then knocked on the door, "Mrs.Noni? Mekhla? Its time to go."

When no one came to the door, and he was too anxious to wait, he urged Julia to go in and have a look.

"Mrs.Noni?" she said peering into the room. "Mrs.Noni, its time to go."

"Go?" Joe heard her ask.

"Yes, its time to go now."

Julia turned to Joe and invited him in once she had

confirmed that the women were proper. He entered the room and saw Mrs.Noni gathering make-up into a kit. Mekhla may have dabbed something on herself but Joe found none of the artificial flaws which he believed make-up would have created.

"Where's Inti?" he asked looking for the raven-haired sprite in a lily-white dress.

"Who?" Julia asked.

"The younger sister, Inti, where is she?" he asked again and called for her, "Inti!"

"I'm in here," he heard her call from the washroom.

"Its time to go."

"Coming," Inti said in a tone that begged for delay from behind the bathroom door.

"Make sure they've packed all their stuff then grab her suitcase," he commanded and approached the bathroom to better hear what the child was doing. "Inti? Are you alright?"

"Yes," she drawled out distractedly, "I'm just getting ready."

"Ok, because its time to go now."

There was a long silence.

"Nooo," the girl lamented and a short scuffle ensued.

"Who are you talking to?" he asked ready to open the door.

"No one," Inti replied sounding relieved, "be right there."

Her voice was promising and he backed away to observe Mrs.Noni struggle with her suitcase.

"Let me help you with that," he said and handily clamped the woman's luggage shut. "Where's their other bag?" he asked no one in particular then turned when he heard the bathroom door open.

Inti pushed her way into the room holding Mekhla's bag slung around her neck reaching and down to her shins.

"Ready," she said beaming beneath her pig tails.

"Here," Joe reached for the bag, "let me take that."

"No, no," she protested, "I've got it. You can carry mother's suitcase."

He was wary that she may fall with the bag tangled around her feet but declined to protest since she seemed so eager to go. Throwing a quick look into the washroom to be certain they were not leaving anything behind he turned to Julia and got her confirmation that the girls were ready. With the suitcase in hand he stood by the door and motioned for them to follow then stepped into the hallway and waited to be certain they did.

"Can I get a saucer of milk with my sandwich today," Inti asked as she carefully managed the stairs.

"What?" Joe wondered, "no, no. No sandwiches today. We're only driving into town. You're going to meet your father. He's waiting for you now."

"Really?" she asked amazed. "Cool!"

Outside, Joe noticed the civvy-clad corpsmen were deployed about the Gas Light's parking lot bent over hedges with assorted gardening tools and acerbic faces overseeing the transfer of prisoners while the same cruel convoy of the day before rested at the edge of the dust ridden lot waiting their turn to mobilize. A slender man in stern business attire stood by the van concealed behind dark sunglasses with a haircut that screamed a military mien louder than any uniform could.

"Inti," Joe said watching her approach the vehicle, "you'll have to sit in the back today. ok?"

"Ok," she replied apparently none-too-distressed.

"Hi, I'm Joe," he said to the stranger in the sunglasses.

"Joe?! and Frank? What are you the fucking *Hardy Boys*?" he laughed derisively, "I never know how to deal with your type. Bogs the hell out of me why I should, but orders are orders. I only hope you don't mess this one up for us."

Ignoring his comments Joe decided to forgo shaking the man's hand and opened the door to help the girls into the van.

"Them the gooks?" he asked.

Mrs.Noni and her daughters shook at the sound of the man's comment but remained passive as they climbed aboard trusting Joe would not leave them in his care.

"No," he replied showing his anger, "these are only the gook's family."

With a forced smile intended to reassure the girls, Joe closed the van's door and took his position in the driver's seat and started the engine.

"I don't know your business, mister, but it'd be best if you kept your tone down until we're done."

"Ah sure," he said, "we got gooks on American soil. I'll be good."

Chapter 20

CHARRED REMAINS

JOE VEERED THE VAN TOWARDS the road and when the brawn bikers braced by the gravel's edge saw that he was ready to go their iron rides roared off the Gas Light's lot. The sun, having seared the day's dew since dawn, made the morning breeze unusually dry as it billowed through the long strands of tangled hair streaming behind the cold blackguard cavalry that led the way towards the city's piers. Gulls flew in the distance and soon the bay's breadth surfaced beneath them in all its placid serenity oblivious of the morning traffic that flowed along its shore. Aluminum albatrosses plunged into port after their trans-pacific flights ready to career and bank back home again with a fresh load and fuel enough for another haul.

Joe's mind drifted with thoughts of the San Francisco Giants who were looking for their seventy-eighth win of the season, as they trekked into Mets-ville New York after splitting with Philadelphia. He stared at Candlestick park letting the dream slip past as the van pressed on beneath the monolithic temple's shadow. The city lay ahead, beyond the highways and thoroughfares gripped with tense motorists commuting through, with its windblown hills and tram-cars where the scene of the beat-generation's wine and poetry feasts made way for the pot and protest fest and the local recruitment grounds for the burgeoning hippie peace cult. The motorcycle engines began to reverberate deafeningly within the city as they announced their arrival with mechanical acclaim bouncing off the steel structured edifices of the downtown core.

All along The Embarcadero site-seeing tourists, pedestrian shoppers and loitering habitués thronging the grounds turned to look at the motor-corps cavalcade as it paraded by until it reached its destined pier where Joe followed the growling iron guard through the gate into a restricted landing area. With Noni's ship moored on the northwest side of the pier Joe placed himself directly between it and the rising sun's glare. Looking towards the deck of the cargo ship, expecting to see the V.C. target, he was disappointed to find no activity aboard. He turned to the port stern, north of the van, where a marine diesel oil truck was tethered to the ship by its thick and heavy fuel line with the driver idly monitoring the process from inside his cab.

"When that sonofabitch steps out you just tell him my name is Green, here talking for Sonny," Joe heard the Company agent sitting next to him grumble.

"Joe?" Inti called to him from the back of the van, "what's going on?"

"It's ok," he said, "we just need to talk to your father," then turning to the man beside him he added, "let's step outside," and opened the door to parley by the van.

A faint gust brought the scent, which every sailor calls the smell of land and every soldier calls the smell of the sea, to their nostrils. While struggling with a near over-powering urge to draw his weapon in a preemptive defense of his shore Green clenched his empty fist and drew himself near Joe to explain his function.

"You're the driver in this operation and now that you've got them gooks here you just make the introduction then shut your fucking mouth and leave the rest to me," he said only looking away from the ship's deck to stare Joe down and conclude with, "you understand me?"

"Yes, sir," Joe replied with military bearing.

Green faced the ship once more and stared it down confident no enemy could escape his constant unblinking vigilance. The van's door handle cracked and the twisting creak of the hinge mingled with the sounds of waters lapping shore but nothing could stir the sullen sentry's icy eyed heed from his commission.

"Come on," Joe said urging the Noni's to escape the stifling heat of the van's confine.

He took the suitcase from Mekhla's slender hand and eased her down then her mother followed and Inti, who still clutched her sister's bag, was lightly deposited next to the pair. As they huddled together near Joe the bearded long-haired biker at the lead of the cavalcade approached.

"They don't board that ship until we get paid," he said blocking them from the vessel.

"I know," Joe replied, "you'll get what you're owed as soon as we make contact with …"

He was interrupted by Green who now talked down to the biker that towered over him, "your presence here poses an undo risk to the successful completion of this mission. You and your men are to remain with your vehicles until this operation is concluded."

"and we're not in the habit of taking orders," threatened the irate road rogue.

"Joe?"

"Not now Inti," Joe hushed the girl and intervened on behalf of Green, "no one's going to let these women board that ship. We're just waiting …"

"Chatrsuda!" The foreign voice calling from aboard the vessel sounded jubilant and elated, "Chatrsuda!"

Mrs.Noni turned to her husband and began to shout in an alarmed fashion waving for him to get away and as she directed her steps towards him Green took hold of her arm and threw her back.

"Get her back in the van!" he said.

"No," the biker caught Mrs.Noni and herded the two others beside her then shouted for his compeers to step forward, "take them to the warehouse. No one's leaving here until I say."

Mrs.Noni struggled vainly to escape while Mekhla slapped the man's arm trying to help her and Inti took refuge behind her savior's leg. As the commotion intensified Joe recognized the soldiers posted on either side of the warehouse taking their positions against the Vietcong smuggler.

"Go with them," he told the child.

"No," Inti begged him to stay with her when she saw Green draw his gun and take aim at the vessel.

"I don't think he'll be in any mood to talk to you now, son," he said by means of dismissing Joe, "take them gooks anywhere that'll get these grease-balls out of my way."

Unconsolable at the sight of Green's gun, Mrs.Noni was taken up, despite her wailing protests, and carried towards the warehouse. After seeing her mother so miserably manhandled

Mekhla was next to be so borne and her younger sister Inti continued to clutch at Joe's leg urging him to pick her up.

"It's ok," he said fending off the burly biker's approach, "I've got her."

Mekhla's bag still hung from her neck and now dangled in front of them as Joe balanced her in one arm and shoved his way along with the other instinctively ducking his head below the live fire which had suddenly erupted around them. They reached the warehouse door expecting it to open but instead found their passage locked and when a simple boot-heel assault failed to run it through the women were dropped to their feet as the bikers renewed their attack more vigorously. Mrs.Noni's first thought was for Inti and as she took her child from Joe she threw Mekhla's bag aside then crouched to the ground to keep the girl safe with her older daughter taking hold of her from behind.

The fuel truck's driver, trapped inside his cab and caught in the battle's crossfire, ground the gears losing his clutch in a panic to race away from the fire fight and tore the ship's umbilical cord allowing the diesel sustenance it fed to bleed across the concrete pier. Eager to break into the safety of the warehouse, the bikers kicked at the door with marine oil purling at their heels, summoning the barking growls of a vicious beast inside. Frustrated with the door they stepped back and fired at the latch unleashing the ravenous fury that bounded out and lashed at the nearest intruder gnashing its teeth as it barked and snapped against the invaders. As the girls were shoved aside by the swing of the door Joe bounced out of the dog's way hearing Inti cry out from behind him.

"No, Peanut! Come back!"

He turned to look and saw the back of her pig-tails hurtling towards a brown spotted kitten that had darted out of Mekhla's bag eager to escape the clutches of the mad dog while the smell of fuel overpowered the rot of washed up waste as the shallow igneous fluid pooled towards them.

"Inti stop," Joe called after her and dashed towards the corner of the building.

Her kitten turned around the building's corner still in a panic to escape the dog's gnashing rabid teeth then was bowled over while trying to stop and escape another yet more fearful threat before dashing away with its ears pinned back in terror towards the gate and The Embarcadero. Gamboling after the frightened feline Inti eluded fire tramping beneath the danger that lurked beyond the corner with Joe still behind her and, as the dog was shot, a city police squad car arrived to halt the cat in its path long enough for Inti to catch it and crouch down to smear its whiskers onto her cheeks with the trim of her white dress resting on the pier.

To protect her from the fire, the patrolman behind the wheel of the squad car parked between her and the conflagration then dove out and snatched her to the safety of the street leaving his vehicle to be engulfed by the flames which now covered the quay and sent up black tar-like smoke. With her head pressed against the police officer's chest Inti could see nothing of the fire-fight that raged on behind them despite the billowing smoke and flames which obscured and distorted the vision of every belligerent. An alert young officer ordered an ad hoc crew of sappers to attack the back of the warehouse seeing to the safety of those trapped inside. When the warehouse flames danced on the building's roof, and the thick black smoke plumed out towards the sky, the gasping combatants crashed their way through improvised exits and escaped the inferno.

Soldiers pulled their lone casualty away from the edge of

the building and doused the fire that had consumed his corpse. As the order to cease-fire quieted the scene, and the enemy had been downed, the only sound competing with the crackling flames were the choking cries of the two women still trapped inside the ruined and crumbling building. The failed attempts to plunge into the blaze and rescue them were hampered by smoke, heat and flames which pushed the seared soldiers back and the ground forces retreated to a safer distance.

"C.I.A.," Green held up identification to the officer overseeing the detention of the three long-hairs that emerged from the back of the warehouse, "let them go."

"I have my instructions."

"You let them go," he shouted then turned to a superior, "these men are friendlies under my jurisdiction."

The order to detain them was rescinded and the gear-guards hurried to their rides.

"Have we got everybody?" he asked, "got them fuckin' gooks this time. Shade, goddamnit where the hell's your man, major?"

"Accounted for," Shade replied while stooped over the charred remains at his feet then standing to his full height.

"And the gooks?" Green asked.

"The women were lost in the fire," he reported to Green's delight.

"Awesome, sometimes things just turn our way don't they," Green brought a cigar to his mouth then sauntered around the flames towards the ship and the soldiers posted there.

"Major Shade?" a policeman approached, "the press will be here soon. If you don't take her now…"

"Yes, thank you officer," he said, "I'll be right there."

Epilogue

Marine pall-bearers, comfortable with the charge of their fallen brother, set the heavy flag-draped casket down onto its supports. Once the chaplain's droning voice had finished calling to remembrance the sacrifices made by yet another selfless son, the non-commisioned officer in charge stepped forward in his crisp uniform, to present arms and summon the three shot clap of the firing party's rifle volley, then retired back to his place as a lone bugler cried taps through his horn a short distance away.

When the thirteenth fold had been pressed and the flag had found its way into the hands of the weary ex-marine, his wife let go of the hand of the dark haired child and a kitten began to play on the lush green grass of Arlington.